PRAISE FOR F

'Fiona Valpy has an exquisite tal
rounded and delightful that they a
makes what happens to them feel very personal.'

　　　—Louise Douglas, bestselling author of *The House by the Sea*

'A novel that will whisk you to another time and place, *The Storyteller of Casablanca* is a tender tale of hope, resilience, and new beginnings.'

　　—Imogen Clark, bestselling author of *Postcards From a Stranger*

'Love, love, loved it . . . Brilliant story, I was completely immersed in it, so moving and touching too. The research needed must have been hard to do but it brought the war . . . to life.'

　　　　　—Lesley Pearse, author of *You'll Never See Me Again*

'A wonderfully immersive novel set against a vivid and beautifully described . . . setting. I loved it!'

　　　　　—Victoria Connelly, bestselling author of *The Rose Girls*

'A moreish story of love, war, loss, and finding love again, set against an atmospheric . . . backdrop.'

　　　　　　　—Gill Paul, author of *The Second Marriage*

The
Season *of*
Dreams

OTHER TITLES BY FIONA VALPY:

The Storyteller of Casablanca

The Skylark's Secret

The Dressmaker's Gift

The Beekeeper's Promise

Sea of Memories

Light Through the Vines (previously published as *The French for Love*)

The Recipe for Hope (previously published as *The French for Christmas*)

The
Season *of*
Dreams

Fiona
Valpy

LAKE UNION
PUBLISHING

Text copyright © 2014, 2022 by Fiona Valpy
All rights reserved.

Published by Lake Union Publishing, Seattle

First published as *The French for Always* by Bookouture in 2014. This edition contains editorial revisions.

www.apub.com

Amazon, the Amazon logo, and Lake Union Publishing are trademarks of Amazon.com, Inc., or its affiliates.

ISBN-13: 9781662503757
ISBN-10: 166250375X

Cover design by Emma Rogers

Printed in the United States of America

tale *(story)*: *n.* histoire *f;* conte *n;* récit *m;* légende *f;*
fairy tale: *n.* conte *m* de fées; histoire *f* à dormir debout;
fairy-tale wedding: *n* mariage *m* de conte *m* de fées;
to tell a tale of woe *(about oneself)*: raconter ses malheurs;
(about others): raconter une histoire pathétique;
to live to tell the tale: être encore là pour en parler;

Chapter 1

The End

Once upon a time, not so very long ago, nor so very far away, an ancient château sat on a hilltop among the vines, high above a golden river.

Halfway through their first season at Château Bellevue de Coulliac, Sara felt she was beginning to get into the swing of the new business. She enjoyed being part of the magic and helping make each dream wedding come to pass in their stone castle perched above the deep valley of the Dordogne.

It was supposed to be picture-perfect, her new life out here in France with Gavin, beginning to build their future, following dreams of their own . . .

So why, in these quieter moments, did she feel such a growing sense of suffocation?

It was a hot summer's night and with a sigh of relief she sank on to the bed and slid her aching legs across the cool sheets. Her nerves were still jangling from the way Gavin had put her down – again – that evening. It seemed to be happening more and more often and she regularly found herself biting her lip, swallowing the words that rose in her throat so that they accumulated in her chest in a big, hard, unspoken lump.

It had been just one more small dig when she was running through the arrangements for the wedding with the caterers. A snide remark about her being such a control freak, that at every celebration there was someone who knew how to put the 'un' in 'fun' and that person was usually Sara. It had hurt and he knew it. Somehow, he always managed to make her out to be the boringly responsible one, while he was the life and soul of the party.

She had tried to talk to him about it in private on previous occasions when he'd made her feel small in front of others. But he'd swept her concerns aside, telling her not to be so petty – that it was just part of the double act they put on for their clients; she should man up and learn to take a joke.

The strain of restoring an ancient French home and building a business had taken a toll on both of them. They'd planned for the renovations, of course – the new roof on the barn, the need to completely rewire the place, the gallons of plaster and paint, and hours of hard work. But they hadn't fully grasped what a bottomless money pit the restoration of a historic building can be, especially in a foreign country where the planning regulations and restrictions were tortuous to say the least. It had been a stressful time, although the sense of achievement still made it all worthwhile.

And, through it all, there had been nothing more guaranteed to focus the mind entirely than the immovable, terrifying, brick-wall deadline of the first wedding of the season looming ahead of them in the diary. It would have been completely terrifying were it not for the fact that she and Gavin were in it together, supporting and encouraging one another through the occasional dispiriting days of that first cold, damp winter with builders' dust clogging every pore of their bodies and their hands blistered and scarred with unaccustomed labouring.

But as she reminded herself of this, unconsciously Sara raised a hand to her throat, as if to soothe the feeling of choked panic that seemed now to have lodged itself there.

It wasn't just the stifling heat and the relentless cycle of arrivals, weddings, departures and then, immediately, preparations for the next event. When she stopped to think, she had a horrible niggling feeling that she'd made a huge mistake. Perhaps the biggest mistake of her life, so far at least. For Sara had burned all her bridges coming out here, selling her tiny London flat and saying goodbye to her burgeoning landscape gardening business, setting her sights firmly on the seductive promise of a sunny future in France, married life with Gavin, a home, a family . . .

She'd taken a chance – a leap into the unknown – when Gavin got down on one knee and proposed not just marriage but a move to France too, and now it was making her feel increasingly uneasy. He'd changed a lot over the past two years.

It was only once the first wedding season had started that she'd noticed that Gavin seemed to need to bolster his own ego by finding fault with her in hundreds of little ways, criticising her efforts and undoing her decisions. Subtly and inexorably, she'd felt her sense of self being eroded. Gavin seemed to have taken over, their partnership morphing into a dictatorship as he began making unilateral decisions, disregarding her suggestions, overriding her plans.

Of course, she told herself, if she was being completely honest it was partly her fault too, for giving in. It felt like when she talked, no one listened. So it had become easier just to do things Gavin's way in the château and instead to channel her own creative energy into the garden, studiously avoiding confronting the sneaking suspicion that the foundations of their relationship were anything less than solid.

Perhaps it was just as well she was kept so busy most of the time, keeping these panicked thoughts firmly at bay. She needed to reserve her energy for the guests, making sure each wedding was perfect.

Every event had its own very particular character, a projection of the personalities of each unique set of participants, and she really did enjoy seeing how each couple stamped their own mark on the proceedings, making their own private fairy tale come true.

Today's wedding had been particularly hard work. The mother of the bride, Mrs Nolan, had been a Fusser, incapable of leaving Sara and Gavin to get on with their side of things, popping up at Sara's elbow at frequent intervals to add some more requests to the already lengthy list of her daughter's special requirements.

'Ever so sorry, but have you got some pink ribbon? Only Brittany wants Melanie to have Bitsy accompany her up the aisle and we've only got the yellow lead with us. And yellow will clash with the bridesmaids' dresses. No, not that pale pink, more of a cerise . . . Oh, well, if that's all you've got, we'll just have to make do. Brittany's not going to like it though.' Eventually, Sara had managed to unearth a length of bright pink ribbon from a drawerful of wrapping paper and Brittany's own personal sun had re-emerged from behind that particular black cloud.

There had been a nerve-wracking moment in the chapel when Melanie, the maid of honour, had lost her grip on the length of pink ribbon tied to the diamante collar of Brittany's handbag-sized chihuahua, Bitsy, and the little dog had made a run for it, almost making it out of the door. Luckily, Gavin's fast reflexes had saved the day and, muttering 'Never work with children or animals', he'd returned Bitsy to the waiting arms and abundantly displayed cleavage of Melanie.

Mrs Nolan was not just a Fusser, she was also a Talker. Sara's ears still rang with the stream-of-consciousness chatter that had accompanied her for much of the day. 'Of course, we wanted Colchester, but Brittany said, "No, Mum, this is my big day, it's

4

got to be somewhere really classy." And with a name like hers, France it had to be. We named her after the place she was conceived, you see.'

'How nice,' Sara responded politely, only half listening as she stacked plates into the dishwasher. 'So you named her after the region.'

Mrs Nolan had looked at her blankly.

'No, love – the ferries. First night of our honeymoon, the crossing from Portsmouth to Santander and then we drove down to the Costa Blanca for a fortnight. Not so many cheap flights in those days, and of course it was before Derek's business had taken off, so there was no spare cash back then. Our little princess doesn't know how lucky she is, off to Bangkok and God knows where for *her* honeymoon.'

We'd better hope her first child isn't conceived on the first night too then, thought Sara, going out to meet the florist and oversee the flower arrangements in the chapel as per Mrs Nolan's detailed instructions.

Mr Nolan, in contrast to his garrulous wife, was a man of few words. He'd made a fortune in the trucking industry, which his wife and daughter were now doing their best to spend. He'd passed the morning sitting in a deckchair in the shade of a cedar tree, with the desperate air of a man who'd been sentenced to deliver a wedding speech for his daughter when he'd really rather be drinking beer in the local bar with the rest of his mates. He'd risen to the occasion, though, and made a fond and funny speech, only once making reference to the dire fate, involving a locked room and a shotgun, that would befall Gary if he didn't look after Brittany in the manner to which she'd become accustomed.

Sara stretched her aching legs and flexed her feet to try to ease some of the tightness in her ankles. The heat was a killer. Every cell in her body throbbed with tiredness. She reached across to set

5

the alarm for tomorrow morning – or, rather, later *this* morning; the clock already showed one forty-seven. She'd been on her feet more or less continuously for – she counted on her fingers – over eighteen hours, and would be up again in five more. But tomorrow would be easier, now that the wedding itself was over; just the Sunday brunch, most of which the caterers would be bringing, and then some of the guests would start to leave, once they'd waved the bride and groom off on their honeymoon. Brittany and Gary would clatter off down the drive, their hire car covered in shaving foam and bedecked with tin cans and inflated condoms, heading for Bordeaux airport and a week on a Thai beach.

She moved her feet again, sliding them on to a cooler patch of the cotton sheet. Having to work in temperatures of thirty degrees or more was draining. When they'd moved here the year before last, Sara and Gavin had sought out the sun, enjoying the novelty of the sensation of heat on their skin as they worked to transform the château into the perfect wedding venue. They'd been so excited: who'd have dreamed that they'd be able to afford this beautiful place? But by scraping together every penny of their combined savings, Gavin's inheritance and the money from the sale of Sara's flat, and by haggling hard on the price, they'd managed it and, miraculously, Château Bellevue de Coulliac was theirs. Next year, at the end of what would hopefully be their second successful season, they'd hold their own fairy-tale wedding in their very own French castle, set among some of the finest vineyards in the world . . .

So, like all the brides she'd seen come and go this summer, Sara should have been fizzing with a sense of joyful anticipation – instead of these feelings of dread, this sense of voiceless suffocation. Not to mention a longing for the comfort of physical affection that had lodged itself under her ribcage like an ache. Of course, it wasn't surprising that Gavin no longer had much time or energy for that side of things; he was working so hard and for such long hours. She tried to remember when they'd last lain together like that, the feeling of his sun-warm skin, his arms, strengthened and tanned a deep mahogany after days spent labouring outdoors, holding her . . .

Maybe things would be different again once they had their first successful season under their belts.

Sara massaged hand cream into her work-roughened hands, easing round her engagement ring, now slightly tight on her heat-swollen finger, and then reached over to switch off the bedside lamp beside her. She'd leave the one on Gavin's side of the bed on, for when he finally made it back to the cottage.

For the wedding season, they'd moved into this basic little stone house, with its one cramped bedroom and single living area with a galley kitchen in one corner, tucked in behind the château next to the walled vegetable garden. At the moment, the walled garden was a jungle of weeds set solid in the heavy clay, which by this stage of the summer had been baked cement-hard, nothing useful growing there other than the ancient, lichen-crusted pear tree in the corner and some herbs that she'd planted in an old stone trough. But Sara had plans to get to work this coming winter to create a proper *potager* with neat raised beds of fresh produce in time for next year's season.

She'd found an ancient notebook in a tea chest full of old documents when they were clearing out the attic. The leather-bound book was a bit tattered around the edges, but its pages held plans for the layout of the gardens alongside lists of plants. It had taken her a while to decipher the handwriting in places – some sections were rain-blotted or written in faded pencil – and she had the sense that this was a real gardener's journal, used in earnest to establish the gardens at the château over a century ago.

In places, the old structure was still visible, but years of neglect had buried the paths and flower beds under a blanket of stinging nettles and the voracious tendrils of brambles. In the end, they'd resorted to using a digger to clear the ground so she could start all over again with a blank canvas, but she'd been determined to use as much of the original layout as she could, so finding the notebook with its sketched plans was a godsend. It was slowly taking shape, recreating the elegant sweeps of planting that drew the eye through the castle grounds to the views across the river valley beyond.

Gavin had relished driving the digger, carving swathes through the weeds and leaving bare earth in his wake. But that was about as far as his interest in gardening went. She recalled the morning when he'd told her the rest was up to her to sort out and gone off to write a few emails inside. That was one of the first times she'd heard that tiny whisper of doubt.

As she lay waiting for sleep to come, alone with her whirling thoughts, the heat seemed to press in on her from all sides. A faint, sulphurous waft of drains hung in the hot night air, a reminder that the sink in the cottage's tiny bathroom was blocked yet again. Their priority had been to get the guest accommodation perfect in the time available: their own summer digs had had to wait, and so things in the cottage were still pretty basic. She'd need to sort the blocked drain out again tomorrow – another task to add to her already lengthy list.

The disco in the barn, which Gavin had been DJ-ing, had fallen silent about half an hour ago, so hopefully he'd join her in bed soon. As long as he didn't settle down with some of the hardier wedding guests and get stuck into another bottle of whisky. It had happened a few times now. When Sara had questioned the wisdom of this – after all, they had to be up early again the next day and back on duty – he'd just laughed and told her that socialising with the guests was an essential part of the business, good for public relations, it was all part of the job. She'd get up first in the morning to set out a few breakfast things for any early-bird guests and leave Gavin to lie in for a precious extra hour or two of sleep.

She gave a little sigh of relief as she closed her eyes, letting the tiredness seep out of her neck and shoulders, her whirling thoughts beginning to settle.

But then she immediately sighed again, with annoyance this time, as someone tapped on the door of the cottage.

Taking a deep breath, she heaved her tired legs back over the side of the bed and pulled on a dressing gown.

'Gav? Sara? It's me, Brittany.'

Sara opened the door to find the bride, in a skimpy wedding-night negligee of peach satin trimmed with black lace, standing on the doorstep. 'Sorry to disturb you so late, only I saw your light was still on. It's Bitsy, she needed a tinkle so I brought her out for a second but now she's run off. I don't know what's got into her, she never does this at home. Could Gavin come and help me find her?'

'He's not back yet, must still be over at the barn finishing up. Come on, I'll help you look. Don't worry, she won't have gone far.' Sara grabbed a torch from the chest of drawers and tied her dressing gown (white cotton, nothing as exotic as Brittany's) firmly round her waist.

They picked their way carefully along the path and then across the lawn, Sara sweeping the torch beam under the trees and into the shrubbery.

'Bitsy! Here Itsy-Bitsy!' called Brittany.

'Shh, better call quietly.' Sara held a finger to her lips. 'Most people are probably sleeping by now.'

They tiptoed on and then suddenly heard a faint yapping, coming from the swimming-pool area.

'That's her!' Brittany's anxious expression relaxed into one of delight.

'Come on, but quietly still, we don't want her to run off again.'

They crept across the gravel path and Sara eased up the latch on the gate in the railings surrounding the pool.

But as she swept the beam of the torch across the paving, she froze in horror, stopping in her tracks so abruptly that Brittany bumped into her from behind. Because on one of the loungers a couple was lying in a particularly intimate position, bucking and gasping as they reached a climax. The torchlight picked out a discarded champagne bottle lying on its side, the crumpled cerise silk of the maid of honour's gown, and then the merry sparkle of Bitsy's diamante collar. The diminutive dog was busily humping the foot of the man who lay on top of Melanie, a foot clad in a distinctive blue, pink and lavender Sebago shoe. And Sara knew, because he referred to them as his Disco Docksides, that the shoe belonged to Gavin, her very own – and now, all of a sudden, ex – fiancé.

Chapter 2

The Morning After the Night Before

There wasn't much that Sara didn't know about wedding etiquette. She had a pile of books on the subject. She knew how to word an invitation, how to draw up a seating plan, the correct side of the church on which to seat the bride's and groom's families. She knew which cutlery and glasses should be used in complicated table settings and she knew (just in case!) the right way to address a duke or duchess.

But what was the etiquette for managing a post-wedding brunch when your fiancé had been caught *in flagrante* with one of the bridesmaids? She suspected that this particular predicament wasn't something she was going to find in any book.

Above all, though, Sara knew that, in this business, the show must go on. Today wasn't about her and Gavin; it was about making sure the Nolans had the event they'd paid for and Brittany and Gary had their happy send-off. So, with a shaking hand, she poured herself another cup of coffee, trying to think straight.

Nightmare! Nightmare! Nightmare! She clutched the sides of her head, then took a deep breath, trying again to get a grip. She needed to shut out the tidal wave of thoughts that kept washing over her in waves of revulsion and panic. Her hands trembled with a mixture of exhaustion and caffeine-fuelled adrenaline as she cupped them around her coffee mug and took another sip.

Startled by the beam of torchlight last night, the pair had leaped up from the sun lounger and Melanie had scuttled off, buttoning up the bodice of her bridesmaid's dress as she fled. Bitsy the chihuahua was still yapping excitedly as Brittany led her away, tactfully leaving Sara and Gavin alone.

Sara reeled with shock and hurt, staring at Gavin, waiting for him to say something. He refused to meet her eye. Almost nonchalantly, he straightened the sun lounger and bent to pick up the empty champagne bottle. His actions were the final straw. Unable to speak, Sara turned on her heel in fury and stalked back to the cottage.

She'd expected him to have the decency to follow her, to apologise and have a proper conversation, in private, about what this might mean for their relationship. But he hadn't, and she had no idea where he'd spent what was left of the night.

She'd hardly slept at all. The image – burned on to her retina – of Gavin and Melanie on the sun lounger made her feel physically sick; her white-hot rage at him for betraying her trust seared her heart; and overlying it all was the humiliation – *Oh, the humiliation!* – and the sheer blind terror at what this meant in terms of her future, her career, her life . . .

It took every last remaining ounce of her strength, but she pushed these emotions to one side and tried to think clearly. After all, the only people who knew were herself and Brittany (though she'd most likely tell Gary, and he'd tell his mates, guffawing with laughter . . . it would already be out there – *no, push that thought aside*) so the best tactic was to keep calm and try to carry on in true British style. Sara would just have to hold her head high, sort out the drinks for the brunch, circulate with the coffees afterwards (and

12

she couldn't help imagining everybody in the room smirking and laughing or – maybe worse still – pitying her).

She slumped her head into her hands again in despair. It was impossible. She couldn't do it alone. Time to use up one of her lifelines and phone a friend.

She reached for the phone and dialled. 'Karen? Yes, it's me. Look, I'm sorry to call you this early and I know it's your day off, but I just wondered whether you could do me the most enormous favour . . .'

◆ ◆ ◆

'Sit. Drink. Eat. And when you're ready, tell.' Sara had never felt so grateful for Karen's down-to-earth, forthright Aussie practicality as she did right this minute. Obeying instructions, she pulled up a chair on the terrace outside the cottage and reached for the mug of tea that Karen had plonked down in front of her.

'Sorry, I might also need to mop first.' Sara fumbled for a tissue and blotted at the tears that suddenly threatened to spill from her eyes. 'Please don't be nice to me, or I won't be able to stop.'

Karen had been fantastic. She hadn't asked for any explanations as to why Sara was calling her at such an ungodly hour on a Sunday morning. She knew her boss well enough by now to understand that it really must be a major emergency and she didn't need to be a genius to guess that something must have happened between Sara and Gavin. In any case, Karen had long suspected that all wasn't quite as idyllic between the couple as it might appear on the surface. She'd noticed how Gavin often sloped off to his office, citing important emails to be answered, whenever there was a job to be done that he felt was beneath him. Sara, on the other hand, was a grafter who'd turn her hand to anything. She really seemed to care for her clients, going the extra mile to make sure each wedding was just what the bride and groom wanted.

Karen had arrived an hour after Sara had called and taken over the brunch arrangements. And when Mrs Nolan had demanded to see Sara about the whereabouts of the box for transporting the top of the wedding cake back to Colchester, Karen had said, firmly and protectively, 'Sorry, she's having a couple of hours off. Let me see what I can find.'

Gavin had avoided Sara completely, but in fact she was thankful for this. There'd need to be a showdown, but it was infinitely better that it should wait until after the guests had gone. She'd glimpsed him earlier, in the distance, cleaning the pool. He'd been talking and laughing easily with one or two of the guests who'd come for a restorative swim. In fact, he was putting on a very good act indeed, appearing smoothly unconcerned as to whether or not anyone knew about his late-night antics. And as she watched from the kitchen window, the horrible realisation dawned on Sara that he had probably had a bit of practice at this . . . those other post-wedding disappearances could well have involved far more than just a nightcap or two in the barn with the last few lingering guests.

Thanks to Karen, Sara had had a couple of quiet hours to try and get her head round what had happened. When they'd moved here, she'd thought her relationship with Gavin was as solid as the buttress of limestone rock on which the château was built. But had it been, really? The niggling doubts in Sara's mind had amplified themselves into a cacophonous clamour as she considered their engagement in light of the previous night's ghastly discovery.

She and Gavin had known each other for just over a year before making the move to France. They'd met when she was planning a landscaping project at a stately home that the events company he worked for was using for a product launch. Her business was starting to gather momentum, with a solid base of regular clients whose elegant London gardens she maintained, and then the occasional bigger project on top, like the one where she and Gavin had met. He'd been growing frustrated at having to work for other people, and was worried, too, that the writing might be on the wall for his job as events budgets were being slashed, the splash-the-cash culture of the City being reined in. He was the one who'd been champing at the bit to get out of London, and he'd talked her into the move, his proposal of marriage finally dispelling any last doubts she may have had about abandoning her business at that stage. ('It'll need to be a long-ish engagement,' he'd said, 'but in the end you can have your own wedding in the château that we've created with our own hands. Imagine that!') And her resistance had crumbled. Because she hadn't realised that while to her the phrase 'let's get married' means 'You are the woman for me: I want you, I need you; I'm in it for life', to Gavin it seemed to translate roughly as 'You seem to be a hard worker: I want your flat, I need your savings; I'm in it for a year or so'.

She'd thought that this time she'd found someone she could genuinely trust. A man different from the others she'd known, one not afraid of commitment. But now, in the bright glare of the French sunshine, with the image of last night's discovery branded indelibly on to her brain, Sara reluctantly admitted to herself that in fact all had not been well in their relationship for quite some time. If they hadn't had the monumental distraction of the move to France, would they have stayed together in London? She had a sneaking suspicion that the novelty had already been wearing off for Gavin . . . It was a classic relationship mistake, wasn't it? Whereas, in a paradoxical attempt to glue things together, some people decide to get married or have a baby, she had sunk her life savings into a terrifying project in a foreign country. It wasn't like her to have been so reckless: usually she was overly cautious where both business and relationships were concerned. But maybe, she now admitted reluctantly to herself, her turning thirty had tipped the scales in favour of making the leap with Gavin.

And she'd always longed – more than anything else – for a home of her own. One of her most vivid childhood memories was of standing at the school gates, long after the last parents had arrived to collect their children, and, as a soft drizzle began to fall, realising that she'd been forgotten. They were all still adapting to the new routine in the aftermath of her parents' divorce, Sara shuttling back and forth between two new houses, neither of which felt like home. It was the first Friday of term and she was supposed to be picked up by her stepmother. So when Lissy didn't show, the eleven-year-old Sara bent down, pulled up her school socks, hefted the heavy bag full of weekend homework on to her back and began to walk. She had no money and the school office was closed so she couldn't go and use the phone there. So she'd walked through the South London streets, head down against the raindrops, which were growing fatter and colder by the minute. As she'd plodded onwards, her bag weighed down her shoulders almost as heavily as the weight on her heart at having fallen through the holes in the family net. She shrank into a shop doorway to avoid a gang of boys, boisterous and noisy with Friday night freedom. Buses swooshed by, their lights bright in the gloom, splashing her sodden shoes with muddy gutter water. She felt in her pockets once again, just in case a miraculous coin or two lurked there to pay her fare, but knowing already that it was hopeless. She picked her way among the other passers-by, purposeful as they made their way home to warmth and suppers, and people who had missed them while they were away.

She'd made a detour to the front door of her mum's new flat, just in case she might be in, even though it wasn't Sara's day to be there. She heard the doorbell echo in the emptiness within but lingered for a few minutes, pressing herself into the shallow shelter of the doorway. The rain was a steady downpour now and she was soaked, the cold raindrops mingling with the warmer tears on her cheeks. She set off again, her shoes squelching down the steps, and carried on through the streets, the last couple of street-lamp-lit miles towards the house where Dad now lived with Lissy and her toddler daughter, Hannah. And with each step, Sara vowed that she would work hard at school and get a job as soon as she could so that she could have her own home and never, never have to be in this situation again. She decided as she walked that she would demand a house key, beg for a mobile phone, save an emergency bus fare from her pocket money and always keep it on her. Sara's fierce determination to be independent and her yearning for a home of her own dated back to that lonely, broken-hearted evening.

She could still remember the look of shock on Lissy's face when she finally opened the door and saw Sara there, bedraggled and forlorn as a drowned kitten. 'Oh, God, I completely forgot. I was supposed to pick you up. Don't tell your dad, will you? He's already stressed out enough as it is with everything that's going on at work and your mum being so unreasonable about the maintenance. Go upstairs and get changed. I'll fetch the hairdryer for you. Hannah, leave Sara alone' – she'd prised Hannah's chubby arms open to free Sara, who was now dripping, most inconveniently, on to the hall carpet – 'and let's go and finish your tea.'

'Lissy, could I babysit Hannah sometimes for you as a job? Be paid for it, I mean?'

'Don't be silly, you're far too young!' retorted her harassed step-mother, even though she sometimes did leave Sara in charge of Hannah when she 'popped out' to the shops.

Sara had gazed out of the dark, rain-rinsed window to the small patch of scruffy grass beyond. Neither Lissy nor her dad had either the time or the inclination to tend to it. 'Well then, could I do your garden? You wouldn't need to pay me much. I can cut the grass and clip the edges. Do the weeding. Maybe plant some flowers for you.'

Lissy peered at Sara quizzically. 'What a funny girl you are! Eleven going on thirty. But yes, okay, if you really want a job then I'm sure we can come to an arrangement. Now hurry up, go and get out of those wet things before your dad gets home.'

So Sara had found her first client, and the coins and then notes – as she'd proved she could do a good job and had taken on the gardens of one or two of Lissy's friends and neighbours – started to mount up, first in a jar under her bed and then in a building society account, quietly multiplying over the years until at last she could afford the deposit for a flat of her own.

Sara shook her head to clear away these old, painful images, kicking herself mentally, angry that she'd been so stupid in gambling away her hard-won independence on Gavin. She'd sworn not to make the same mistakes her parents had; their divorce and subsequent respective marriages stood as more stark, unhappy milestones on the path of her childhood.

And now the irony wasn't lost on her: she'd only been to two weddings before they'd bought the château – when her mother married her stepfather and her dad married Lissy. Fairy-tale endings and happy-ever-afters? Not in her bitter experience. Which had made it an even greater leap of faith for her to accept Gavin's proposal, lured by the promise of a dream home and a dream wedding of her own. But it looked as if she'd simply walked straight into another monumental mistake, all of her own making. Well, she'd certainly had it with marriage now, she thought angrily. Even if, irony of ironies, she did have to make her living out of arranging other people's weddings.

Karen pushed the plate of biscuits towards her. 'C'mon, Sara, you've got to keep your strength up.'

They could hear a cacophony of shouts and cheers from the parking area: the bride and groom were about to depart and the brunch guests were seeing them off. And then people would start to drift away, back to the guest houses and holiday villas where they'd been staying, or off to catch flights or to start the drive northwards, leaving only the Nolans and a core of close friends and family who were staying in the château that night and would be departing in the morning.

'You sure you don't want me to stay and do tonight's supper?' Karen asked, patting Sara's hand.

'No, I'll be okay now. There aren't going to be many people left and it's just a cold buffet. You go home now and enjoy what's left of your Sunday afternoon. See you on Tuesday morning.'

'Sure you don't want me to come in tomorrow?' The entire team at the château normally had Mondays off to recover, before making a start on the preparations for the next weekend's wedding.

'Don't worry, I'll be fine. The rest of the guests will be out by mid-morning. And I guess Gavin and I have some serious talking to do . . . And, Karen, thanks for today.' Sara's throat caught and she stopped to wipe her eyes again and blow her nose.

'No probs, my dear, all in a day's work.' Karen patted Sara's hand. 'Tell you the truth, I can't say I'm all that surprised this has happened. Since the season began, I've watched you fading away into the background. Gavin seems to . . .' – she hesitated as she searched, tactfully, for the right words – '. . . throw himself into his work, but it's often looked like it was at your expense.' Sara thought she understood Karen's careful, coded message. Perhaps her growing suspicions about Gavin's post-wedding activities were accurate.

Karen smiled encouragement, reaching for her handbag and car keys. 'Now, you'd better go and wash your face and slap a bit of camouflage on those eyes before you go up to the château. *Bon courage*. And see you Tuesday.'

◆ ◆ ◆

19

Gavin kept a low profile while there were still guests in the château – she didn't know and didn't care which empty bedroom he'd found to sleep in. Finally, once Sara had waved Mr and Mrs Nolan off down the drive, their Range Rover packed to the gunwales with Brittany's wedding gown and veil, the bouquet, the remains of the cake, and Bitsy's pink-velvet-lined travelling case, she made her way back to the cottage to try and unblock the sink, carrying a plumber's plunger in one hand and a large adjustable spanner in the other. She found Gavin there, stuffing clothes into a duffel bag.

'Sorry, Sara,' he muttered, head down, not looking at her. 'I just can't do this any more.'

'Do what, Gavin? The work on the château? The wedding business? Or our relationship?' Sara was amazed at how calmly she spoke, like a parent speaking gently and reasonably to a recalcitrant child. She felt numb. He'd now strayed so far off the path of reasonable human behaviour that she didn't seem to be able to come up with an appropriate emotional response. Or maybe it was simply a defence mechanism kicking in so that she could deal with the bare essentials of the situation in which she now found herself, her mind automatically shutting out the waves of anger, terror and pain that had washed over her again and again over the last two days.

'Any of it,' he mumbled, grabbing the keys to his car, not meeting her eye. Then he paused, straightening up to look at her as she stood there with the plumbing tools in either hand. 'This was a mistake. I'm just not ready for the commitment.'

There it was again: the 'c' word. Her worst fears realised, suddenly a pulse of pure fury surged through Sara's veins. '*Is that it?*' she shouted, brandishing the plunger as though it were the sword of truth. 'You're leaving, as easily as that? What about the business? What about the future? What about us?'

'Sorry. I just have to get out of here. I'll be in touch.'

A white-hot pain blinded her, a potent hit made up of equal parts of fear, anger and grief possessing her body, taking over her actions, faster than thought.

Her right arm drew back and then, with every shred of her wordless fury and frustration concentrating itself into that one reflexive action, she hurled the heavy forged-steel wrench at his head.

Adrenaline may have greatly boosted her strength, but it did nothing for her aim and Gavin easily dodged the missile. Gathering momentum as it spun through the air, the wrench crashed into the wall behind him and there was a dramatic explosion of splintering wood and pulverised plaster as the old, crack-riddled surface disintegrated in a cloud of dust.

Shocked into silence, Sara stood motionless, horrified by her own action and its explosive outcome.

Without a word, without even turning to look at the damage behind him, Gavin bent down to pick up his bag and walked out into the sunshine, leaving her standing there, shaking, as the dust cloud settled slowly to the floor.

She heard him start the car and drive away, the fading sound of the engine drawing her, stumbling, through the doorway of the cottage, along the path to where the château slumbered, oblivious, in the afternoon sunshine.

She stood, stunned, the tinnitus scream of summer cicadas loud in the silence. A faint cloud of dust, kicked up by the wheels of Gavin's car, floated in the air above the drive. As she watched, rooted to the spot, it drifted away, leaving only a shimmer of heat and the surreal sense that her life for the past eighteen months had been nothing but a magical illusion, one that had now disappeared in a puff of smoke.

She pressed a hand against the carved cream stone of the château's cavernous doorway, to steady herself and to reassure herself that something solid and tangible still remained. The sun-warmed blocks of limestone emanated a sense of peace, and history, and imperturbability. She thought of the hundreds of others who must have passed through this doorway down the centuries, and gathered strength from the thought that they would have lived out their own personal tragedies and triumphs within these ancient walls. Could she transform this disaster into a triumph of her own? Or would she have to beat a retreat, returning, defeated, to try to resurrect the tatters of her old life and her old business back in London?

She rested her aching forehead against the stonework for a moment, craving the comfort of the building's strong embrace, as a child craves the security of its parents' arms, gathering strength from its solid presence. Then, on shaky legs, she made herself walk back to the cottage to find a broom and start cleaning up the mess.

It looked as if it had snowed. A fine layer of plaster dust coated every surface in the single room that served as kitchen, dining and sitting room. Her footprints made tracks across the worn floor tiles as she went to inspect the damaged wall. The jagged ends of brittle laths, eaten away by woodworm over the years, framed the sizeable hole where the plasterwork had collapsed so explosively. Dustpan and brush in hand, Sara set to work, trying to focus on clearing up the wreckage of the wall rather than contemplating the wreckage of her life.

Once she'd swept up the debris, she began to wipe off the remaining film of plaster dust. Mopping alongside what was left of the wall, she noticed that the hole had exposed a bundle of old rags, presumably packed in behind the wooden laths as a crude form of insulation when the wall had been plastered originally. Back when materials were scarce and costly, people stuffed all sorts of things behind walls to pad them out. During the restorations in the château they'd found wads of old newspapers dating from the

1920s, and the barn walls had been packed with bundles of straw that looked as though they'd been nested in by rats.

She fetched a black bin bag and then took hold of a corner of the tatty material and tugged gingerly, trying not to let any more pieces of broken plaster fall on to the newly washed floor. Suddenly, with a slither of sleek fur and a sinuous undulation of its thin, rubbery tail, a mouse leaped from the rags and scuttled away under the kitchen units, making Sara screech in fright and revulsion.

'It's only a little mouse,' she admonished herself, her voice loud in the silence. 'Come on, girl, get a grip.' She picked up the metal wrench and hooked the end of it under the rags, lifting them out carefully in case any more rodents lurked in their grubby folds.

The fabric appeared to be mostly old moth-eaten blankets, but one of the pieces was darker than the rest. She pinched the rough black worsted between thumb and forefinger to pull it from the tangle. Then, with another reflexive shudder of horror, she dropped it on to the floor. She could hardly believe her eyes. The whole day seemed to have turned into some surreal nightmare from which she feared she might never escape. Because there on the damp floor, like a dark ghost, lay a black military jacket. On one of its sleeves was sewn a badge in the form of an eagle with its powerful wings outstretched. And in its talons, clearly distinguishable, the silver threads glinting dully under their covering of dust, the eagle gripped a laurel wreath encircling a stark, geometric form that made Sara gasp again: the unmistakeable outline of a Nazi swastika.

Dizzily, as the blood rushed to her head, Sara reached out a hand to steady herself against the kitchen units, feeling as though the walls were collapsing in on her metaphorically now, as well as literally.

She'd looked upon these buildings as her allies, their ancient stones reassuringly solid, and she had drawn strength from the sense of benevolent history they seemed to exude. But now she felt a sense of unease creep over her. She'd been living alongside this hidden jacket. How on earth had it got there? And what else might these walls conceal?

During the course of the building work in the château, she'd come across piles of mildewed newspapers alongside the tea chest in the attic. More ancient history was written into the weathered beams, the rough stone walls, the time-smoothed grain of the polished wooden floors. But they'd found no other evidence of the war years, despite the fact that Château Bellevue had stood here through both world wars. Sara knew that this particular area of France had seen its share of the horrors as much as anywhere else in the country. She'd seen the discreet monuments, dotted here and there on the streets of Sainte-Foy-la-Grande, marking the places where members of the Resistance had fallen. But people didn't seem to want to talk much about those dark times, keeping the memories firmly locked away from the light of day and, on the rare occasions when she'd had the chance to ask, no one had been forthcoming about the part the château had played in it all.

Looking more closely at the jacket lying on the floor in front of her, she realised it must have been the mouse's nesting material of choice as it was completely eaten away in places. Despite being so threadbare, as well as the eagle-and-swastika badge, one lapel sported another emblem picked out in the same silver thread, a double lightning flash forming two angular letters: SS.

Sara shivered, despite the warmth of the early evening air. Panic rose in her throat once again as a tangle of thoughts and images in her head threatened to suffocate her. Everything had its dark side. She'd been blissfully ignorant of Gavin's infidelities, but he'd betrayed her trust. And now the very walls surrounding her, which had once felt safe and solid, seemed to be turning against her, taunting her with secrets of their own.

Get a grip, she warned herself. *Losing it is not an option.* Gathering her inner strength, she briskly picked up the jacket and shoved it into the bin bag along with the tattered blankets that she'd pulled out of the wall space. She swept up the last few fragments of plaster, gave the floor a final wipe with the mop and then, determined now, feeling surer of herself, she caught up the bag of rags and a box of matches and marched out into the walled garden. In one corner, the furthest from the old pear tree, she raked together a pile of dried weeds and sticks. Then, as the setting sun cast the dark shadow of the walls across the ground towards her, she knelt and set a match to the tinder. A bright flame licked its way along a slender filament of grass, flickered doubtfully for a moment as it met a dry twig, then caught, drawing in air, gathering strength. Sara felt her own strength growing with the flame, her recent anger, fear and revulsion feeding it, helping her shake off her former sense of suffocation.

Perhaps Gavin's departure was the best thing that had happened to her in a long while.

She pulled the jacket from the bin bag and bundled it into a ball, setting it on top of the blazing sticks so that it would catch. The fire licked at the wing tips of the silver eagle, before starting to devour the swastika. She watched, making sure the emblem was completely consumed, before feeding the rest of the tattered blankets into the flames. And as the smoke rose into the night sky, she stretched her arms above her head, breathing deep, finding her voice had returned with Gavin's departure. 'Good riddance to bad rubbish,' she said out loud, her words flying upwards with the sparks and disappearing into the darkness.

She watched until the fire had died down completely and then poured the contents of a full watering can over the smouldering embers to make sure they were safely extinguished. Clapping the ashes from her hands, she closed the gate of the *potager* behind her and then stood for a moment, defiant in the darkness, surveying the cluster of buildings slumbering before her.

She'd invested so much in this place . . . In terms of physical hard work, she'd grafted on the buildings, lovingly repointing stonework, sanding and lime-washing beams, painting walls in colours that glowed with serene depths of tone befitting these ancient rooms. With the help of Claude, their part-time gardener, she'd laboured in the grounds as she reclaimed the original structure, carving out a logical flow of paths and beds from the bare clay, digging in tons of compost to improve it so that she could establish her planting schemes. Now, soft carpets of prairie plants interspersed with obelisks of English roses and silver-leafed olive trees drew the eye towards the sweeping views beyond.

In financial terms, she'd risked every penny she had on a future that had seemed to have such a good chance of succeeding when the two of them were committed to it, but now seemed distinctly tenuous. And emotionally, she'd invested everything she had too: her hopes and dreams, her love, her trust. In the darkness, she took stock, steadying herself against the castle's walls, sensing its ancient foundations solid beneath her feet, taking a deep breath.

Okay, so the emotional investment was a write-off. Gavin's behaviour had ensured that there could be no way back on that score. But she had the château, with six more weddings booked through August and the beginning of September. Daunting though it seemed, she'd just have to manage without him. Thank goodness she had the support of such a good team. And then, at the end of the season, the château could be sold and she would return to London and try to pick up the threads of the life she'd left there. She just needed to get through the rest of this summer . . .

Back in the cottage, she stood under a lukewarm shower until the plaster dust and the smell of smoke from the bonfire were washed from her hair and skin. She lay down on the bed, loneliness her only companion, and the silence closed in around her.

But then, in the quiet darkness, a tiny scuffling sound from the living room next door made her sit up and listen. The mouse had returned to the space behind the wall and was busily making itself a new nest, rebuilding its ruined home. She smiled to herself. It was quite nice to have the company.

And if that mouse could do it, then surely she could too.

◆ ◆ ◆

Sara smiled in turn at each member of the company gathered around the kitchen table. 'So that's the situation, I'm afraid.' She'd decided that there was no point trying to whitewash it. 'Gavin's gone back to England.' (Had he? She had no idea, but it seemed the most likely scenario. He'd probably have run home to that bossy mother of his – and of course she'd be delighted to have him back. 'Goodness me!' she'd exclaimed on first meeting Sara. 'She's really quite petite. You said she was a gardener. I was expecting something a bit more Amazonian!' Sara suspected no one would ever be good enough for Mrs Farrell's golden boy.)

'But I think we can manage, as long as you're all sure you're happy to do a few additional shifts?'

'Suits me,' nodded Karen. 'The extra money will come in handy.'

Twin sisters Hélène and Héloise Thibault exchanged a glance and nodded. 'It's good for us. We need to save up for university next year anyway. We'll earn more money and have less time to spend it – it's a win-win situation.' The girls lived in the local village of Coulliac and had just left school. Gavin had always referred to them as the 'Héls Belles', a nickname that had stuck.

Antoine, the sommelier, bartender, waiter and general dogs-body, shrugged. He was a student of winemaking at the university in Bordeaux, and the only member of the team to live on-site, in what used to be the piggery but was now a bright studio apartment. 'I'm here anyway and the weddings are my social life. It's no problem.' This was quite a long speech for him. He'd been taken on for the season as he spoke both French and English fluently, as well as for his knowledge of wine and ability to mix a mean Bloody Mary, but he appeared to be a man of few words in either language, flushing bright scarlet whenever addressed directly. And especially, Sara had noticed, when in the presence of the Héls Belles.

'Okay, great. Let's focus on this coming weekend then.' Sara handed each member of the team a photocopied programme with details of the next wedding and their shifts. She pulled her glasses down from where they perched on top of her head and scanned the programme. 'So it's a pretty straightforward one this time. The house party here Thursday to Monday, the wedding on Saturday afternoon, the usual timing for the service and then straight on into the photos, drinks and meal. Antoine's on the bar. The florist will be in first thing on Saturday morning and the caterers will be in after lunch to set up. Henri Dupont is taking the photos, so he knows the form.'

'*Ooh là-là!* Better wear our steel knickers, girls,' laughed Karen.

'I know, I know,' Sara sighed, shaking her head. 'But he does take a good photo. And he's local. And not completely extortionate when it comes to pricing. We aren't exactly spoilt for choice.

'Now, any questions, anyone? Then let's get started on the bed-rooms. Hélène, can you give the windows in the big sitting room and the snug a clean, please? And Héloise, could you do a pass with the feather duster to get the cobwebs off the beams? I noticed a couple in the barn.' It was a relief to focus on the business in hand, moving forward to the next event.

'Don't worry, Sara, we've got it under control,' said Karen, beginning to sort bottles of cleaning materials into four buckets.

Sara re-scanned the papers on the table in front of her. 'The only thing I haven't managed to sort out yet is a DJ. I don't suppose any of you know someone locally who might be able to stand in for the next six Saturdays? I'll have to ring round and see if anyone's free.'

Karen whistled through her teeth. 'That's not going to be easy at such short notice and at the height of the season. Can't you just set a playlist running?'

'Not really.' Sara picked up some stapled sheets from the pile of papers. 'Gavin was really good at tailoring the music for each wedding. It makes all the difference between a so-so party and a great one.'

Just then they were interrupted by the sound of a vehicle pulling up at the kitchen door, its radio blaring out 'Let Me Entertain You' at full volume. Karen glanced through the window and turned to Sara with a grin. 'Well, well. What a coincidence!'

The music was switched off as suddenly as the van's engine and there was a tap at the door. '*Coucou! Le vin est arrivé!*'

'Aha! Thomas, the very man,' said Karen.

'*Oh là-là.* I used to think the British had the worst French accents in the world, but now I know it's the Australians. How many times do I have to tell you, it's To-*mah*. The emphasis on the second syllable; no "s".'

'Okay, okay, Tommy-boy, keep your beret on! Honestly, you French are always so nitpicky.'

Karen and Thomas both laughed and then he began unloading the delivery of wine from his family's vineyard in the next valley over, Château de la Chapelle. As Antoine helped him carry the boxes into the cellar, Karen nudged Sara. 'Why don't you ask him to DJ? He'd be ideal,' she whispered.

'D'you think he might do it? I hate to ask him. He's probably too busy.'

'Beggars can't be choosers. And anyhow, now is the quiet time for winemakers. They leave the vines alone for the last few weeks leading up to the harvest so the grapes can ripen naturally.' Karen's husband had a workshop that maintained agricultural machinery, so she had her finger on the pulse of the local farming community. 'Ask him,' she urged again. 'You've got nothing to lose.'

Thomas came back into the kitchen with the paperwork for the delivery. He was a good-looking guy, the easy-going second son of Château de la Chapelle's owner, and Sara always enjoyed his cheerful visits when he came to deliver their wine orders.

'Would you like a cup of coffee?' she asked in as nonchalant a tone as she could manage. 'We were just about to have one.'

'*Volontiers.*' A slow, easy smile, warm as French summer sunshine, spread across Thomas's face. 'Is Gavin here? I wanted to explain something about the invoice to him.'

'I'm afraid he's not. And in fact, I want to ask you something . . .'

Thomas's expression changed to one of sympathetic concern when he heard Gavin had gone. Sara tried to keep it light but, however calmly and minimally she outlined it to Thomas, there was no disguising the fact that the situation in which she now found herself was a serious one, given that half her annual income depended on delivering the next six fairy-tale weddings to a standard that would meet – or preferably exceed – the expectations of her clients.

Thomas had been leaning forward, elbows spread on the table, his capable hands clasped around his coffee cup as he listened to Sara talk. He was a good listener and she could tell he understood there was more to Gavin's abrupt departure than she was prepared to divulge.

When she stopped, he leaned back in his chair, running a hand through his jet-black hair and stretching his legs in front of him.

That slow smile spread across his face once again, softening the angularity of his aquiline features.

'*Eh bien, pourquoi pas?* My brother and his family are at the beach for the next few weeks while the vineyard is quiet. And my job is much easier these days anyway, now that we have Gina selling our wines into the English market – she's the wife of a good friend and a real expert with wine. If I stay in on Saturday evenings, my father will make me play card games with him and drink too much *pastis*. And, on the other hand, you are asking me to come and be the DJ for wedding parties attended by hundreds of hot English girls. Hmm, it's a difficult decision, but yes, okay, I'm prepared to sacrifice my precious weekends to help you out. On condition that you buy huge amounts of wine from Château de la Chapelle. And maybe your wedding guests would like to come and do a tasting with us and buy even more wine to take home with them? This would be good business all round, I think?'

Sara reached out a hand. 'It's a done deal,' she said, shaking his firmly. 'You're a complete star, Thomas, I can't tell you how grateful I am for this. Antoine, could you show Thomas the barn and all the kit?'

The two men left to go and play with the sound and lighting system, and a few minutes later party music was blaring out across the courtyard, startling the swallows out of their nests under the eaves of the barn.

Sara turned to Karen, beaming with relief. 'As easy as that! It's nothing short of a miracle.'

'Seek and ye shall find,' grinned Karen. 'Oh, and by the way, something you'll learn about living here in rural France? When a neighbour is in need, people step in and help out. It's one of the few advantages of everyone knowing your business.'

'It's so kind of him too. What a lovely guy. I've always liked him.'

The Héls Belles glanced at one another and giggled, and Karen assumed an expression of mock exasperation.

'*What?*' asked Sara in all innocence.

Karen came over to her. 'I think perhaps the time has come to take off these *Engaged Goggles*.' She carefully removed Sara's reading glasses, folded them deliberately and placed them on the kitchen counter. 'And then we need to loosen up the *Strictly Taken* hairdo,' she continued, easing the elastic band off Sara's tightly pulled-back ponytail, letting her glossy dark hair tumble over her shoulders.

'Hey!' Sara protested weakly, and Hélène and Héloise giggled harder.

'And finally we need to loosen up the *No-Fly Zone* modesty shield.' Karen undid a couple of buttons at the neck of Sara's blouse.

'There,' she said, stepping back to admire her handiwork. 'What d'you reckon, girls?'

'*Pas mal*,' laughed Hélène.

'*Much* better,' declared Héloise.

'You see, in case you hadn't noticed, thanks to the force field you'd erected around yourself as Gavin's loyal fiancée, Thomas is a man. And not only that, he's a French one. And rather a cute one too. And he might not have been quite so ready to take on the role of DJ if you weren't a very attractive and suddenly single woman of roughly his own age, in an area where people matching that description are somewhat few and far between.'

'Oh Karen, that's rubbish! I'm sure he's only interested in the business opportunity. It does make sense to sell his wines to our guests.' Sara blushed. 'Anyway, shh now! He's coming back.'

She smoothed her hair behind her ears as she went out to meet him.

'That's a fantastic sound system!' he said. 'And the lighting looks really professional – the glitter ball's a great touch. I'm looking forward to making my debut on the decks this weekend. If it's okay, I'll come back for an hour or two on Thursday afternoon before your guests arrive. I want to make sure I've got the hang of the systems and set up a playlist or two. And what time do you need me to come over on Saturday?' Thomas's natural enthusiasm for life reminded Sara of the bubbles in a glass of champagne.

'About six thirty? We'll give you a plate of dinner in the kitchen too if you like? Thanks again, Thomas, you're a lifesaver.' She deliberately kept her back towards the kitchen door, conscious that Karen and the Héls Belles were watching this exchange intently.

Thomas leaned in to kiss her on both cheeks and she inhaled the faint fresh-baked-bread scent of his warm skin, suddenly acutely conscious of the muscularity of his clean-cut jawline. 'It will be my pleasure,' he said gallantly, that slow smile lighting up his face again. 'I'm looking forward to it, Sara.'

She waved, watching as he drove off down the drive. Karen came out to stand beside her and, without turning, Sara murmured, 'He really is quite cute, isn't he?'

'Attagirl,' Karen said with an approving nod. 'It's good to see you getting straight back out there.'

Sara shook her head. 'I was only joking,' she laughed. 'There's no way I'm ready to even think about another relationship. But thanks for thinking he might find me vaguely attractive, Karen – you've made my day! Anyway, once this season's over, I'm going to turn the château into a nunnery and appoint myself the Mother Superior. No men allowed, ever again. I've learned my lesson. Now, let's get to work. We've got bedrooms to clean and loos to scrub.'

Chapter 3

Niamh & Keiran

Mr and Mrs Pádraic O'Callaghan
request the pleasure of your company
at the marriage of their daughter

Niamh

to

Mr Keiran Best

at Château Bellevue de Coulliac

On Saturday 4 August
at 3.30 p.m.

RSVP
Greenways, The Oaks, Straffan, County Kildare

Sara began to chop the vegetables for a ratatouille to accompany tonight's supper, hot oil sizzling in a pan on the stove beside her. The smell of frying onions and peppers filled the château's cavernous kitchen.

She threw in garlic, courgettes and tomatoes and, as she stirred the fragrantly steaming pot, she gazed out of the kitchen window across the courtyard to the barn where Thomas was testing the lights and practising on the decks and Antoine was un-stacking chairs in preparation for Saturday night's hooley. The château and its clustered buildings were peaceful in the afternoon light: the calm before the storm. The golden stone gently reflected the sunshine's warmth, and the courtyard's borders of Iceberg roses and lavender softened the edges of the gravel paths, the whole Impressionist effect forming the perfect romantic backdrop for a fairy-tale wedding.

Gavin used to say that their job was making dreams come true. The reality, as Sara well knew, was that achieving it demanded a heck of a lot of hard work, an eye for the minutest of details, and most of all the ability to keep calm in the face of demanding wedding planners, difficult guests, plumbing disasters, alcohol poisoning, overexcited children, overexcited groomsmen, hysterical brides, hysterical mothers of brides, family fallings-out and every other drama that weddings entail.

And those challenges paled into insignificance against the test of abandonment mid-season by one's business partner, let alone one's husband-to-be. She supposed she should still have felt bitter at the thought of organising dream weddings when the prospect of her own had just disappeared over the far horizon with its tail between its legs. But – honestly? – she found to her surprise that she felt okay. In fact, she was almost relishing the prospect of making a success of the business on her own. She realised she was regaining her self-confidence, finding her voice again, her independence. Running the business single-handed was going to require her to get it back fast and she felt a new sense of certainty as she went about her work, as if, having picked herself up from such a painful fall, she was getting back into her stride more surely than before.

She pushed a strand of hair back from her forehead. In this heat, the pots of verbena and geraniums would need watering this evening – she'd better remind Antoine. She swept the vegetable peelings into the compost bucket and made her way out to the walled kitchen garden, where the weeds were parched in the summer heat. She had planned that this time next year neat rows of produce would be burgeoning in raised beds, with an automatic watering system to ensure the rich clay soil stayed soft and hospitable. She felt a pang of sadness, realising that it wasn't going to happen now. Next year seemed an impossibly long way off: the château would belong to someone else by then . . .

A squadron of swifts screeched overhead in the dizzy blue of the August sky. She took a deep breath, relishing the last few moments of peace. As she bent to pick a generous bunch of pepper-scented basil from the stone trough, there was a low hum from the speakers in the barn and then suddenly The Pogues' version of 'The Irish Rover' blasted out: Thomas was rehearsing his welcome for the guests. Sara smiled. This was the overture: time to go and raise the curtain – the show was about to begin.

◆ ◆ ◆

A convoy of hire cars wound its way up the drive, dust billowing in the evening air. Sara identified the O'Callaghans – the friendly, larger-than-life parents of the bride, with whom she'd been in frequent communication over the previous few months – and went to introduce herself. Amid the hubbub of laughter and excited chatter, she managed to allocate the guests to their rooms, Antoine and the Héls Belles helping to show them the way. Vast suitcases were dragged from the backs of the cars and manhandled into the house.

Sara always thought you could tell within the first five minutes what the family dynamic was going to be. This one was good, so she felt her shoulders relax slightly: fewer inter-family tensions meant fewer fires to put out.

Niamh, the bride, was luminous, a natural Irish beauty with dark blue eyes and delicate, creamy skin. Her happiness radiated from her like the sun, and the rest of the company orbited around her, keen to hug her, carry her bags, laugh with her and bask in the warmth of her joy. And Keiran, the groom, was a handsome rugby-playing banker who clearly doted upon his girl. Of course, that was usually (though not always) a given: if the bride and groom weren't obviously in love with one another at this point in the proceedings, then there really was trouble ahead. More often, it was the dynamic between the two families where potential problems lay and Sara's radar usually tuned in to the relationships between the two sets of parents. Here, it seemed, there was a genuine fondness already. The two mothers were deep in conversation about a mutual friend, who had scandalised the local community by finding herself a toy boy. And Sara knew, because she'd helped arrange it, that the fathers of both bride and groom were in the group going off to play golf tomorrow morning as part of the pre-wedding activities; it turned out they were members of the same golf club back home in Ireland.

She led the O'Callaghans to their room, carefully carrying the large cardboard box that contained Niamh's wedding dress.

'Once you've settled in, you'll find drinks on the terrace. Let me know if there's anything else you need. There are hangers here,' she said, opening a wardrobe, 'so you can get this hung up as soon as possible.'

Mrs O'Callaghan sank on to the bed, gratefully kicking off her shoes. 'Will you look at my ankles; they've swollen to twice the size in this heat.' She fanned herself with her passport.

'Well, you're here now, so you can relax this evening and recover. Make yourselves at home. I'll see you downstairs shortly.'

Sara left them to unpack and went down to the kitchen to start the pork roasting for dinner.

The château slept twenty-four people, plus extra children if necessary, so tonight there'd be two tables of twelve. The kids could eat at the kitchen table and then go and play outside, until their slightly tipsy mothers tore themselves away from the dinner tables to get them into bed. It was a system that worked well, meaning everyone could relax and enjoy themselves.

'Who's a lad got to shag to get a drink around here?' Liam, the best man, came into the kitchen and put a beefy arm round Sara's shoulders.

Sara grinned. 'Well, your best bet would be Antoine. But otherwise there's wine and beer out on the terrace. Help yourself. And take these with you as blotting paper.' She handed him a plate of cheese straws and a bowl of nuts.

'By God, you know the way to a man's heart, Sara. Sure, it's a crying shame you're already claimed or I'd do it myself.'

She shooed him out of the kitchen, knowing full well that one of the best man's duties was to flirt with every woman there, from the youngest flower girl to the mother of the bride and every other female in between. She let him believe she still had a man – the picture of her and Gavin was still up on their website – it was easier and more professional that way. But the line of paler skin on the fourth finger of her left hand was less distinct now, as time and the sun's golden rays erased the last vestige of their engagement.

The sound of laughter wafted in from the terrace. The easy friendliness of this crowd was going to make this wedding an enjoyable one; it sounded as if they'd already made themselves at home.

Friday morning dawned with a clear blue sky, promising that the weather was one thing Sara could cross off the list of potential glitches for the weekend. Karen had offered to do the croissant run – usually Gavin's responsibility – on her way to work, coming in a little earlier than usual. Breakfast was easy and relaxed. Thankfully, here in France no one expected a full British fry-up. Sara switched on the coffee machine, set the oven warming and quietly washed and dried the glasses from the night before. She went down to the cellar to fetch more supplies. The cavernous space beneath the kitchen made a good larder, with its rough stone walls hewn out of the bedrock. Tempting though it was to linger there for a while, cocooned in its cool quietness, she sorted briskly through what was needed and carried packets of cereal and a crate of summer fruits up the narrow staircase. The children would be down early, no doubt, and need fuelling up, ready for a busy day in the pool.

Sara perched on a stool beside the kitchen counter, sipping a cup of strong coffee topped up with steamed milk and scanning the weekend's programme, checking and rechecking the details against the contents of a plump folder marked: *O'Callaghan-Best*. She'd learned to keep a record of every email, telephone conversation, quote and invoice so that there could be no possible room for confusion or misinterpretation. Today's schedule involved golf for some of the party, wine tasting for another group and the option of a canoe trip for the older children and those who wanted the exercise. Some would stay relaxing by the pool or reading in the shade, of course. And tonight there were extras for dinner as members of the extended family on both sides, who were staying in guest houses and hotels in the local area, were invited for the rehearsal dinner. It was to be a buffet of *charcuterie* – cold meats – and quiches with salads, which Karen and Hélène would help her prepare this afternoon. Straightforward enough.

She slid the typed programme back into the file and stood up as the sound of children's voices wafted down the corridor. 'In here for breakfast,' she beckoned them, to allow the heavier-headed of the late-night revellers to sleep it off a while longer . . .

◆ ◆ ◆

Later that day, Sara lingered for a few more moments, her feet propped on the edge of a stone planter to ease her aching calf muscles, before hauling herself upright from the deckchair where she'd been grabbing a few minutes' rest after a quick sandwich for lunch in the cottage.

Car engines could be heard pulling into the car park, then doors slamming and the chatter of golfing stories being exchanged. Sara noticed that a few of the men had taken out a rugby ball and were throwing it back and forth. She thought she'd better try and manoeuvre them tactfully away from the cars and into the big field where there would be less scope for dented bonnets and splintered windscreens. As she made her way across to them, the wine-tasting party pulled in and the volume of noise grew as the flock of flushed girls emerged from their minibus. Clearly, they'd had a good time.

Sara was just reaching the post-and-rail fencing at the edge of the parking area as the bride's brother, Robby, a fellow member of the groom's rugby group, wound up to spin the ball across to Liam. There was a dull thud, a shocked silence for a split second and then a scream from Marie, the chief bridesmaid, as Niamh staggered back against the minibus, clutching her face. The ball had hit her full on and for a moment she swayed as if losing consciousness. Keiran was across the parking area in three long strides, his arms around his stunned bride, while the bridesmaids rounded on Robby. 'You eejit, what in the hell d'ya think you're doing?' He hung his head in shame, ducking their scolding.

'Niamh, are you okay? Speak to me!'

Sara waited on one side while Keiran tried to pull Niamh's hands from her face, stooping to peer at the damage. As she took her hands from her eyes, there was another scream from Marie at the sight of a trickle of blood. Sara fished a clean tissue out of her pocket and passed it to Keiran, who pressed it tenderly against the wound.

'I think it's just a scratch, not deep.' But Sara could see that the eye socket was already a deep red where the corner of the rugby ball had caught it a glancing blow. A bride with a black eye was not going to look good in the wedding photos.

'Come on, let's get you back to the house. I've got a first-aid kit in the kitchen and we need to clean that up.' Sara led the way, Keiran and Robby solicitously helping Niamh. One of the children had already run on ahead with the news and the fearsome sight of Mrs O'Callaghan steaming round the corner of the chapel was enough to make the sturdiest of rugby players tremble in his boots. 'Now, Mother,' said Mr O'Callaghan, holding up a hand to fend her off, 'it was an accident is all. She'll be okay in a moment.'

'Robby O'Callaghan, I'll skelp you, so I will,' fumed his furious mother.

'It's all right, Ma,' said Niamh, the tissue still pressed against the side of her nose. 'Nothing a bit of make-up can't hide.'

In the kitchen, Sara ran cold water on to a clean flannel and handed it to the mother of the bride to gently clean her daughter's wound. It had stopped bleeding now, thank goodness, but Sara was right; the eye socket was beginning to swell and turn an angry red. Mrs O'Callaghan kept up a stream of lament about thoughtless boys who'd no doubt had a pint or two too many at the golf club, and why hadn't Mr O'Callaghan had the wit to stop them?

'Keep that cold cloth pressed against it for now, it should help stop the swelling,' Sara advised.

'Don't worry, sis – if the worst comes to the worst, there's always Photoshop,' contributed Robby helpfully.

Sara turned to shoo away Robby, Liam and the gaggle of concerned bridesmaids who were crowding around the kitchen sink. 'Why don't you go outside to the terrace and I'll bring some tea? I think we could all do with a cup,' she said, smiling at the bride's mother in an attempt to prevent further O'Callaghan blood being spilt. Tea and cake were always a useful distraction in tense situations, she'd found, helping to soothe frayed nerves and re-bond fractured relations.

◆　◆　◆

A couple of hours later, Sara and Hélène were finishing up the dinner preparations in the kitchen and Antoine was loading up trays of glasses for setting out on the terrace for the pre-dinner drinks, when Mr O'Callaghan popped his head round the kitchen door. 'Could I take a glass of ice water up for Niamh?'

'How's she doing?' asked Sara solicitously.

He shook his head. 'Putting a brave face on it in public. But she's just been having a wee weep on her mother's shoulder in the privacy of her own room. It's a shame for her big day and all, but worse things have happened at sea. She's got a proper shiner developing though, right enough. She's upset at facing everyone for the rehearsal dinner tonight, never mind her wedding day tomorrow.'

'Poor girl. But it'd take more than a little thing like a black eye to mar her natural beauty.' Sara shook her head. 'Hang on a sec, though,' she went on. 'I've an idea that might just help. Can you get Liam and a couple of the boys rounded up?' She checked her watch. 'We've half an hour to go . . .'

And so when Niamh O'Callaghan, soon-to-be-Best, arrived at the terrace door to make her entrance to her rehearsal dinner, her

42

black eye concealed as much as possible by make-up and her head held high, her handsome groom handed her a pair of sunglasses. 'You'd better put these on,' he said.

She shook her head. 'It's okay, Keiran, I'm grand.'

'Well, fine then, if you want to be the only one left out, that's all right by me.' She shot him a quizzical – and slightly lopsided – look as he put on his own pair of sunglasses and offered her his arm. And then she stepped on to the terrace, where every single member of the assembled company, including the youngest baby, the oldest great-aunt and each member of the waiting staff, was sporting their own pair of dark glasses in solidarity with the bride.

Niamh's lovely, bruised face broke into its habitually radiant smile as the penny dropped and then, laughing and crying simultaneously – which played complete havoc with her make-up – she put on her sunglasses and plunged into the loving uproar as the entire room erupted in spontaneous applause.

Sara breathed a sigh of relief. Another crisis averted. All in a day's work in the wedding business.

◆ ◆ ◆

'. . . and so it only remains for me to ask you all to join me in raising your glasses in a toast to the beautiful bridesmaids!' Liam's speech had gone down well and Sara breathed a sigh of relief that the more nerve-wracking parts of the proceedings were now over.

The bride's black eye, which had turned a dramatic shade of purple overnight, had been thoroughly dabbed with concealer and powdered into near oblivion, and luckily the worst of the swelling had subsided. The photographer, Henri Dupont, had done his best to take photos that made the most of Niamh's unspoilt profile. Sara kept a beady eye on him. He was good at his job but seemed to feel that one of the perks that came with it was the opportunity to do a little extracurricular close-up work with whichever bridesmaid or luscious wedding guest seemed either the most drunk or the most obviously available. Whenever he looked as if he was about to carve one of the girls off from the throng and inveigle her into the shrubbery, Sara would attempt to intercept him with a request for more photographs of the top table. She now realised how ironic it was that she'd been so distracted trying to keep tabs on Henri's behaviour that she hadn't noticed Gavin was engaged in similar pursuits, right under her nose.

It had been a lovely ceremony. Like most of the weddings that took place at Château Bellevue de Coulliac, it was a service of blessing that had taken place in the old deconsecrated chapel off the west wing. To keep things simple, most couples usually had a small civil ceremony at home beforehand, so that they'd be legally married in their own country of residence, and then in France a blessing of some sort and an excellent party afterwards. With the desserts now over, the best man was asking everyone to make their way to the barn for the cutting of the cake and the bride and groom's first dance. Sara was always interested to see what each couple would choose for 'their song', which Thomas would have prepared as the opener on the playlist for this evening. He was taking his new role seriously and had spent hours on Thursday afternoon compiling the list, trying to include as many requests as possible, keen to get the music right for his first wedding.

As the lights were dimmed and the glitter ball started to revolve, 'The Way You Look Tonight' began to play and Niamh smiled up into the loving gaze of her besotted husband, the two of them completely oblivious – for a few moments – to the loving throng of friends and family who beamed at them from the edges of the room. Then Liam and Marie, Mr O'Callaghan and Mrs Best Senior, and Mrs O'Callaghan and Keiran's father took to the floor to join them.

Thomas was doing a brilliant job. He'd taken to his DJ-ing duties like a duck to water. Sara leaned against the barn door, watching him from the shadows. Before now, she'd always simply thought of him as a business colleague, one of the many suppliers they dealt with. But Karen was right: he really *was* a very good-looking guy, with his dark eyes and generous grin flashing in the disco lights. As if sensing her eyes on him, he glanced in her direction and, catching sight of her, his face lit up with that slow smile again and he raised a beer bottle in salute. He seemed to be in his element. Blushing in the darkness, and thankful that he couldn't read her thoughts, Sara smiled back and gave him a thumbs up.

The music segued into a lively Thin Lizzy number and there was a surge on to the dance floor. Antoine was already mobbed over at the bar, pouring whiskies with both hands. On her way to help the caterers fold the last few tablecloths, Sara stopped in at the kitchen to put a few more bottles of water in the drinks' fridge: they'd probably be needing them tomorrow.

◆　◆　◆

'Goodbye! Good luck! Have a wonderful time . . .' The assembled company had gathered to give the bride and groom a send-off as they were about to climb into the convertible they'd hired and head for the airport and their honeymoon flight.

Niamh and Keiran came to find Sara, who was dispensing ice lollies to the children. 'Thank you for everything. You made our wedding so perfect,' said Niamh, as she and Sara embraced.

'Well, speaking of perfection, Henri has said he can touch up the photos if you want him to. He'll send you preview copies and you can let him know if you want any airbrushing done on your poor eye.'

The new Mrs Best smiled up at her husband. 'You know, I think we'll leave them just as they are. It'll remind us of this wonderful party, and that you have to take the rough with the smooth in life. What really matters is family – no matter how annoying some of them may be sometimes – and friends. And us being together.'

'Yeah, and I quite like the front-row-of-the-scrum look on you. You wear it a lot better than most props I know.' Keiran hugged her to him.

Sara joined the other guests to wave the pair off from the front steps of the château, then turned to go back in and brew some more coffee to take round as the party wound down.

'I've got a really good feeling about that pair, you know,' said Karen with an approving nod, carrying a tray of crockery in from the terrace.

'Yup. That's going to be a happy-ever-after one, I think.' Sara began to wash up a few extra coffee cups.

Niamh's parting words echoed in her ears: *You have to take the rough with the smooth in life.* And Sara realised Niamh was right; there was no point trying to airbrush reality. She'd been able to get through this wedding mostly by avoiding thinking about Gavin's departure, which had resurrected so many painful memories of abandonment from her childhood. Now she felt able to face the fact that what they had was over; but at the same time, she wouldn't be here were it not for him. It came as something of a revelation. She felt a wave of acceptance break over her, washing away the terror she'd had of facing the rest of the summer alone.

'Here,' said Karen, nudging her away from the sink with her hip. 'I'll wash, you dry. Well, that's the first one flying solo safely over.'

Sara nodded. 'Thanks to all of you. One down, five more to go this season. You know what? I think we might just be able to do this.'

Chapter 4

SOMETHING NEW

It was her favourite moment in the week: those perfectly peaceful hours just after the last wedding guest had departed, when she had the château to herself. Even when Gavin had been around, Sara would purposefully take herself off into the garden every Monday at midday, to savour the calm beauty and the rare luxury of being alone for once. She took a deep breath and let it out slowly, a long sigh of relief at having another event successfully crossed off the list, another sizeable cheque banked, the money to cover the next round of salaries and bills safely stashed away.

She'd expected to feel lonely with Gavin gone, but had discovered to her surprise that she really quite liked her own company. In fact, paradoxically, she realised that there had been times when she'd felt more lonely with him *around*. As her confidence had ebbed, she'd found herself deferring to him in most matters to do with the business – after all, he was the one with event management experience, and he was also the majority shareholder, having had the inheritance from his father to invest. But now, instead of seeing herself as one half of an engaged couple, she was suddenly a complete entity in her own right again. It was as though she'd been holding her breath since their engagement, and suddenly found she could breathe freely once more.

She stood gazing out at the view and drank deep the warm air, faintly perfumed with dust and the scent of lavender. A pair of pale-blue butterflies danced about her head, dizzy with the joyful abundance of summer, intoxicated by the garden she'd planted for them on this magical hilltop.

As she watched, a white van making its way along the road in the valley below the château turned in at the gate, bumping up the drive. It couldn't be the laundry van, which called on Tuesdays to pick up the weekend's sheets and towels and to drop off fresh ones for the changeover. Nor was it Claude, the gardener. Perhaps it was someone from the catering company who'd left something behind. Taking her time, reluctant to break the spell of those few perfect moments, Sara came across the courtyard to find Thomas Cortini waiting for her.

'Thomas! What a fantastic job you did on Saturday night. The guests loved the party – lots of them said how great the music was. You're a natural!'

'*Ah bon*, I'm pleased that you're pleased, Boss. You've got a great set-up here. I hadn't realised before how much work you and Gavin have done on the old château. It's good to see it restored to its former glory.'

'Thank you. That means a lot, coming from someone who's lived around here all his life.'

'Anyway, Karen tells me that Monday is a day off here. And as I was passing your door on the way back from dropping my father at the airport, I thought I'd call in and see if you'd like to come for lunch. I've brought a picnic.'

'Oh, that's kind of you, Thomas, but I really should be getting on with a few phone calls about arrangements for the next wedding.' Sara's default response was a protective one. (And then it occurred to her to wonder why he and Karen had been discussing when her day off was . . . Sara suspected a certain Australian matchmaker just might be at work here.)

Thomas, not about to take 'no' for an answer, tapped his watch. 'But, Sara, *c'est midi*. Everywhere will be closed – if they were even open in the first place on a Monday in August! And if I might remind you,' he continued, mock officious, 'under the regulations governing the thirty-five-hour working week here in France, employees are obliged to down tools for two hours and go and sit by the river and eat bread and pâté. It's also compulsory to drink a glass of chilled wine, in order to support your local *vigneron*. Your phoning can wait until later, when people will have returned to their desks in a very good humour thanks to their long and reviving lunch break.'

She laughed and shook her head. 'Well, if you put it like that . . .'

'And if you do not comply, I may have to report you to the union for being in contravention of the rules.' Thomas clinched the deal.

'What did you say your day job was again? Something about sales and marketing? You're very good! Give me two seconds to go and grab my sunglasses.'

In the cottage, Sara ran a comb through her fine, dark hair and swept a little colourless lip gloss over her lips.

'Where are we going?' she asked as she climbed into the van.

'Not far at all,' replied Thomas.

True to his word, he pulled in at the gates of an old mill, which sat on the riverbank less than a kilometre from the château. 'This is my sister-in-law's parents' house,' he explained. 'I'm keeping an eye on it while they're away on holiday at the Bassin d'Arcachon for a few weeks with the rest of the family.'

He hauled a picnic basket out of the back of the van. 'You can carry this' – he handed her a freshly baked *baguette*, still warm from the baker's oven and wrapped in a twist of brown paper – 'and I'll bring this.' He picked up a wine cooler. '*Allez, viens!*'

He led the way past the front of the ancient stone mill house and along a narrow path that led to the river, one of the smaller tributaries of the Dordogne. A weir had been built across the river and, on the nearside, a narrow channel of water had been diverted so that it plunged and foamed under the old mill wheel, at rest now after its centuries of work, the sluice gates beside it standing open to allow the water to flow through freely. They settled themselves in the shade of a generous-limbed willow tree that trailed its leaves languidly in the slow-flowing water below the weir.

Sara gave a small sigh of contentment. 'Amazing. These are practically my neighbours and I didn't even know this place was here. What a lovely spot.'

Thomas busied himself setting out plates and unwrapping little greaseproof parcels of pâté and cheeses. He drew the cork from a dew-misted bottle of white Bordeaux from Château de la Chapelle and poured a little into two glasses.

Sara held hers up appreciatively. 'Proper glasses too, I'm impressed!'

'But of course. Only a philistine would drink such a wine as this from plastic. *Santé!*'

He tore a generous chunk from the *baguette* and put it on one of the plates, handing it to Sara. '*Sers-toi,*' he urged.

Suddenly ravenous, Sara spread a thick slice of pâté on to the bread and bit into it. She hadn't felt much like eating since Gavin left, and in any case it hardly seemed worth the effort to cook anything for one. *Funny how congenial company is by far the best seasoning for any meal*, she reflected.

'So you were taking your father to the airport?' she prompted.

'Yes, he's off to England for a few days. At the age of nearly eighty, he's found himself a lady friend there. *C'est génial!* I haven't seen him on such good form since my mother left him fifteen years ago. He's learning to play bridge and drink tea. It's given him a whole new lease of life.'

'And your mother? Do you see her often?'

'*Oui, de temps en temps,*' he shrugged. The gesture was a casual one, but Sara noticed how his normally sunny demeanour appeared to change as he talked about his parents. His shoulders tightened and there was a defensiveness in his tone, beneath the deliberate nonchalance. 'But she's often busy with her stepfamily. She remarried, you see. Her husband's a dentist in Bordeaux, retired now of course.' Sara nodded sympathetically: she knew all about stepfamilies, having two of her own. He continued, 'She doesn't like coming back to the vineyard. A guilty conscience, I suppose. The *vigneronne*'s life was never really for her; she's a city girl at heart. She was always restless living here in the countryside.'

Something in the way he said this made Sara glance at his face, trying to read his expression. 'So are you more like your father or your mother, do you think?' she asked, sipping her wine.

He sighed, and allowed his shoulders to drop as he set aside his plate. When his eyes met hers, there was a new openness in them, one that had been concealed by his determined cheerfulness until now. 'Honestly? In my heart of hearts, I suspect there's a lot of her in me. My brother, Robert, is just like our father. He's a winegrower through and through. Papa always says wine runs in our veins in the Cortini family. His own father came here from Italy to work in the vineyard and then fell in love with the daughter of the owner of Château de la Chapelle. So our family's link with winemaking goes back generations. The expectation is that we will naturally stay in the business. But I don't think I have the same commitment to it that Robert does.'

'Don't you enjoy your job? You're very good at it.' Sara kept her tone deliberately light, not wanting Thomas to retreat behind the defensive wall of his habitual persona. She was starting to understand there were hidden depths beneath his handsome, happy-go-lucky exterior.

'It's not that I don't enjoy it. Just that . . .' He paused, and picked a few crumbs from the crust of his bread, then threw them into the water, enticing a flurry of tiny silver fishes to the surface.

Sara sat still, gazing at the river, giving him time.

'Well, it's just that I feel there's a whole wide world out there that I'd like to explore.' His eyes shone as he turned to look at her, his face lighting up again. 'I have – how do you say it in English? – the feet that itch. Up until now, though, I've always been tied to the vineyard, having to be there to support my brother, who loves his vines and making the wine, but detests having to sell it.'

He offered Sara a triangle of creamy Brie and topped up her glass.

'But now things are changing,' he continued, his eyes still shining with a new expression of hope. 'Gina Thibault, the wife of a friend of mine, is helping to sell our wines and she has good links to the UK market. Sales are booming, so my job is much easier. With more money coming in, I may be able to start making some trips abroad. Try to develop new markets. And, if it continues to go well, I could take time off to go travelling. I'm planning on starting early next year – not that I've told my father and brother that yet. Leaving will be hard, but by next spring I should be out of here if I can make it work. Who knows, I might even find somewhere I love and live overseas for a while. It will broaden my horizons, for sure.'

'Sounds great!' Sara grinned at him. 'It's funny . . . Your dream is to leave here to travel the world. And my dream was to move here to see a bit more of the world. I suppose adventures must always depend on your starting point.'

'And what about you?' Thomas handed Sara a perfectly ripe peach and she sliced into it, the sweet juice pooling on her plate. 'Will you continue with your business here in France on your own?'

Sara shrugged. 'I'm not sure. All I can think about at the moment is getting through the next few weeks to the end of the season. Once the weddings are finished for the year, I should have more time to take stock. It'll depend, too, on what Gavin does next. If he wants his money out of the business then I'll have no choice but to sell the château.' She was careful to keep her tone light, but surprised herself with the dawning realisation that she didn't want to have to sell after all.

'And how would you feel about that? That would be a shame, *n'est-ce pas?*' What was it with this man? He seemed to be able to read her thoughts, the real, deep-down, essence-of-Sara thoughts, not just the ones she chose to present on the surface.

She hesitated, watching a leaf swirl slowly by on the surface of the water, considering another throwaway reply to try to deflect him. But something about Thomas's own honesty made her decide to let down her guard.

'You're right, I'd be gutted. At first, I thought I just wanted rid of it – too many associations with Gavin and the way he's treated me. It's funny, though, having got through that last wedding without him, I now realise how much I love this place. Too much to give it up without a fight. All that hard work . . . and I still have plans for the garden that I'd like to see through. I feel Château Bellevue somehow deserves to be given an elegant setting that's worthy of its history – not that I know much about it, but, living there, I get the sense of very many lives lived before us and, hopefully, many more to come down the years. I suppose it makes me aware of how transient we are, while the rocks and the stones remain. I'd like to make my mark here. Leave something behind when I'm gone.' She turned and smiled at him. 'Sorry, I'm wittering. That's what comes of plying me with wine at lunchtime!'

He shook his head. 'No. It makes sense. And you're right – it has a long history, although what's real and what's just rumour is hard to unpick. The previous owners claimed just about every king and queen from Henry the second and Eleanor of Aquitaine onwards slept there at one time or another. There have been many weddings in the chapel down the centuries – you are continuing that. There's even rumoured to be a secret tunnel, full of ghosts, that runs from this very mill up to the cellars of the château!' He opened his eyes wide, in mock fear.

'How exciting. I'll have to look out for that,' Sara laughed.

'Actually, there could be some truth in it. The limestone around here is honeycombed with caves. In Saint-Émilion they've got a whole church underground. And you've probably heard of Lascaux, over past Bergerac, where there are caverns full of fabulous prehistoric cave paintings. Look.' He pointed to where a small stable door was set into the rock face behind them. 'They've even got their own small cave here. There are no prehistoric paintings in it though, just their lawnmower!'

Sara decided to tell Thomas about finding the Nazi jacket in the wall at the cottage (although she carefully edited out the bit about throwing the wrench at Gavin's head) and he nodded slowly, thinking. 'I did hear something about the château being occupied by Germans in the war. There are many such stories around here, although they are seldom told. It is really a time that people would rather forget. So many terrible things happened. It was complicated, being an occupied country, and it tore communities apart. You English have the luxury of not having been subjected to that. It's probably difficult for you to understand.' Thomas shrugged and smiled, signifying a change of subject, closing down that particular conversation in the way people usually did around these parts. He'd piqued her interest, though. Perhaps the tea chest full of old ledgers and documents would hold a few more clues to the château's history. She determined to find the time to have a look through them properly when she got back.

He clambered to his feet, brushing off a few crumbs, and held out a hand to her. 'Come! It's time to have a go at walking on water.'

'What do you mean?' Sara looked towards the top of the weir, a line along which the deep-flowing brown river water suddenly transformed itself into a rushing sheet of shallow white rapids that swept down the slope into the more peaceful pool in front of them. 'You surely don't think I'm going to walk across that?'

He grinned, hauling her to her feet. 'Come on, it's perfectly safe.'

He led her across a little bridge of turf-capped stones and on to a small island between the sluice channel and the river. They kicked off their shoes, leaving them at the foot of a broad-trunked oak tree, and Thomas stepped down on to the top of the weir. Long strands of golden-green weed trailed just under the surface of the water like mermaids' hair. Sara hesitated, then took the hand Thomas was holding out to her and stepped, gingerly, into the water. She'd expected the stones to be slippery, but the weed formed a rough mat, which her feet gripped easily. The rushing water was shallow, scarcely up to her ankles, and refreshingly cool. She relished the feeling of the hot sun on her arms and the cold, clear water flowing over her feet.

They walked out, slowly, into the middle of the stream, titanium-blue dragonflies hovering about them. One landed on her bare shoulder, light as a wish, resting there for a moment before launching itself once more into the rainbow-filled air over the weir.

In the centre of the river, they stopped, the stones firm under their feet, a deep brown pool on one side of them and the frothing slope on the other, where the mermaids' hair disappeared beneath a foaming bridal veil. As the water gushed around them and under them, Sara turned to face Thomas with an expression of pure delight. 'Oh! It's wonderful! Thank you for showing me this.'

He looked into her eyes. 'Here's to adventures, wherever we may find them.' He leaned towards her and then, for a fleeting second, his lips brushed hers, as light as the touch of a dragonfly's wing.

Before she had time to respond (or even to think what the correct response should be), he turned and, with a whoop, leaped into the deep brown river above the weir, disappearing beneath the water.

'Thomas!' she cried, frantically scanning the river. 'Thomas!'

He resurfaced upstream, five long seconds later, his hair sleek as an otter's, grinning broadly.

'Dive in, Sara!' he called. 'Push away from the wall towards me and pull hard; that way you'll be safely clear of the faster flow.' She hesitated and he beckoned, treading water. '*Allez, viens!* It's wonderful!'

Oh well, what the hell, she thought, and leaped, diving smoothly into the unknown depths and pulling against the drag of the river's powerful embrace. She too resurfaced, gasping at the combined effects of the chill of the deeper water and the flood of adrenaline that coursed through her body like quicksilver.

Side by side, they struck out for the bank, hauling themselves on to the grass on the far side of the river. They collapsed, gasping and laughing, the sun immediately starting to warm their goose-pimpled skin and dry their wet T-shirts and shorts.

Sara sat up. 'Thomas Cortini! Isn't it dangerous to swim near a weir?'

'Of course. You have to know what you're doing. But this river is small and slow-flowing enough, as long as you're over this side and keep away from the sluice.' He sat up beside her, hugging his knees, and gave her a sideways grin. 'Anyway, you jumped too. You obviously trusted me!'

'It wasn't that at all. It was just because I thought you might need saving,' she retorted, mock primly. She combed her fingers through her wet hair. 'Lucky my watch is waterproof.' She glanced at the time. Gone half past two. But suddenly she found she didn't care about the time for once, and she flopped back on to the grass, closing her eyes against the bright sunshine. On this side of the river, the roar of the sluice was hushed. Fluting, liquid birdsong floated through the canopy of branches above them. They stayed like that for a while, side by side, in companionable silence, allowing the warmth of the dappled sunlight to soak into their skin.

Finally, Thomas got to his feet and offered her his hand. 'Ready to walk back across?'

As they packed up the picnic things, Sara shooed a couple of wasps away from the sticky plates. Thomas winced defensively as one flew in his direction. She laughed. 'Not scared to dive into a fast-flowing river, but frightened of a tiny wasp?'

He grimaced. 'Ah, you've discovered my Achilles' heel, I am indeed a coward. But with good reason. I'm allergic to their stings.'

'Better stand back then and let me do this.'

He smiled. 'Are you always so independent and capable?'

'When I have to be, yes.'

'In that case, I have no doubt that you are going to stay on at Château Bellevue and make your business a huge success,' said Thomas, suddenly serious.

'Well, I shall expect you to send me postcards from all over the world,' Sara replied. 'And Thomas? Thanks for today. For sharing this beautiful place with me. It was just what I needed.'

That evening, alone in the cottage, Sara spread a selection of the documents from the tea chest on the kitchen table. There was what looked like a ledger, bound in burgundy leather with a gold cross embossed on the cover, and in it she found a register of weddings that had taken place in the chapel. The earliest one dated from April 1859. Recorded in sepia copperplate ink, each entry noted the names and addresses of the bride, groom and witnesses, along with the name of the priest who'd presided. There were gaps in the dates here and there, which, she realised, largely coincided with the two world wars. But on either side of these there appeared to be more ceremonies than usual – only natural in the run-up and aftermath, she supposed. The most recent marriage recorded was in 1945. A local girl called Eliane Martin had married one Mathieu Dubosq. After that, the entries stopped and there were only blank pages.

After a moment's thought, Sara reached for a pen and her folder with details of the weddings they'd already held in the château that season. She left a page between the modern day and the past, then carefully wrote the names of the latest couples to be married in the chapel into the book. It gave her a sense of satisfaction to see them there, a sense of playing her part in continuing a history that had had its upheavals and its times of darkness, yet which still showed that love endured.

She sighed, thinking her own wedding might have been recorded here too, had those dreams not been shattered. But being the custodian to these hopes and dreams for others somehow buoyed her spirits.

She made herself a mug of mint tea and then opened a dog-eared album of old photographs she'd also excavated from the tea chest. There were pictures from the turn of the twentieth century showing men dressed in tennis whites and women in long dresses wielding croquet mallets. A few of them had names and dates written underneath. She imagined one of the young men might have been the last Comte to reside at Château Bellevue – Charles Montfort – whose name she knew from a memorial plaque set into one of the chapel walls along with the dates 18 November 1877 – 6 June 1944.

Sara pored over all the pictures, particularly the ones that showed aspects of the garden in its heyday. Her newly established planting schemes seemed to be along the right lines, in keeping with the originals but with her own twist of modernity here and there. She could only imagine the colours of the roses, but the drifts of purple lavender would have been the same as those lining the paths today.

Among the later photos were a few in colour, taken in the walled garden. She moved the album closer to the light to be able to see them more clearly. There was the pear tree in the corner. Beneath it was a series of beehives and in front of them stood a girl wearing a cotton apron and a broad-brimmed hat. Her long, straight hair was streaked blonde and, from beneath the brim of her straw hat, she seemed to be gazing beyond the camera, her expression serious. Written beneath it were the words: *Eliane at work in the potager, May 1938.*

She turned back to the page in the ledger where the final wedding had been recorded all those years ago. Was this Eliane Martin? The same girl who'd been married seven years later? She wondered what her life would have been like during those seven years, when France was overwhelmed by war and occupied by the enemy.

Sara glanced at the hole in the wall – still awaiting a plasterer to come and fix it – and remembered the Nazi jacket that had lurked there. There was so much she didn't know about her new home. If only walls could talk . . .

Then she tidied the ledger and photo album away, but left the file of this summer's weddings sitting on the table. She switched off the light and went to get ready for bed. Tomorrow was another early start. There were preparations to be made. And in a few days' time there'd be another marriage to record in the ancient ledger, continuing the tradition that had begun all those years ago.

Chapter 5

Matthew & Hamish

MATTHEW *and* HAMISH

Invite you to come and help celebrate their union

On Saturday, the 11th of August
At 4.30 p.m.
At Château Bellevue de Coulliac, France

RSVP
55 Northumberland Place
Edinburgh EH3 5LR

Thomas looked bemused. The team was assembled around the kitchen table for the Tuesday morning briefing and Sara had just handed him the request list for Saturday's event.

'What is the "Gay Gordons"? And "Strip the Willow"? And then we have a "Foursome". And then, *mon Dieu*, an "Eightsome"! When I signed up to be your DJ, I didn't think I'd have to get involved in anything like that. *Oh là-là*, there have been rumours about what you English get up to at these parties at Château Bellevue, but I never imagined they were really true!'

Antoine and the Héls Belles were also looking a little alarmed.

Karen guffawed. 'Never been to a gay wedding before then, Tommy-boy?'

'Don't worry, Thomas.' Sara patted his hand comfortingly. 'It's Scottish dancing. Hamish and Matthew want to kick off the party with some reels, which are a type of Scottish folk dance. It's fantastic – you're going to love it. One of their friends is going to be the caller, to tell everyone the steps. All we have to do is download some Scottish dance music. I'll help you find what we need.'

Sara scanned her notes. 'Hamish and Matthew are entering into a civil partnership in Edinburgh. But because that's not exactly romantic, they're also having a ceremony in the garden here, to re-exchange their vows in front of their friends. Then it's drinks, dinner, dancing, as usual.

'Antoine, could you go and collect the champagne this morning?' she continued. 'They've ordered the very best, Louis Roederer Cristal, 2004. And vast quantities as well. Matthew Humphreys is an up-and-coming fashion designer and he evidently has an eye for perfection. Everything about this party is going to be stunning. Right, everyone happy with their shifts for the weekend? Then let's get to work.'

As Karen and Sara stripped beds, bundling the linens into big canvas laundry bags, Karen asked nonchalantly, 'So, Sara, what did you get up to on your day off yesterday?'

Sara smiled, remembering. She kept her voice deliberately casual. 'Oh, nothing much. You know. The usual.'

Karen nodded. 'The usual. Hmm. That's very interesting, because my husband saw you and Thomas Cortini turning in at the old mill when he was on his way home for lunch. So if that's the "usual" then I think there's something you need to tell me.' She shook her head. 'It's always the quiet ones . . . And as they say, still waters really *do* run deep.'

'Oh, my God! Can't a girl get away with anything around here?'

'Nope. If you so much as sneeze, people will be calling round with their own special cold remedies and a pot of chicken soup. Especially an *Anglaise* who's been recently abandoned in her hilltop château, which happens to be one of the area's most prominent landmarks. You are currently the source of much local entertainment and speculation in Coulliac. Of course, it's lucky for you that I am the soul of discretion and loyalty and would never divulge to the gossips a word of what really goes on up here.'

'Well, unfortunately for me, very little *does* go on up here.' Sara peeled off a pillowcase and plumped the pillow emphatically, adding it to the pile of bedding airing on a chair before the open windows.

Karen raised an eyebrow, pressing her lips together tightly, as if she knew otherwise.

'What's that look for?' demanded Sara.

'I'm saying nothing. Like I said, I'm the soul of discretion . . .'

Sara looked at her suspiciously, thinking. 'Well, it's not me. And the only other person up here is Antoine.'

Karen pressed her lips together even harder, suppressing a smile.

'You don't mean . . . ? But who . . . ?'

'All I'm saying is you're not the only one to have romantic assignations with members of the opposite sex.'

Just then, Héloise popped her head round the bedroom door. 'Sara, is it okay if I accompany Antoine to the wine merchant's?

He might need some help carrying the champagne? I've finished stripping the beds in the three end rooms and the laundry van will only be here with the clean linen in an hour.'

'Yes, of course, Héloïse. That's fine.' Sara kept a straight face until Héloïse's footsteps had clattered safely down the stairs and then she and Karen burst out laughing.

'My goodness,' said Sara weakly, 'it must be all this exposure to weddings. Love certainly is in the air.'

Just then, Thomas popped his head round the doorway. 'Can you come and help me choose the Scottish music, Sara?' He grinned. 'I have found something called a *Highland Fling*!'

He turned to go, and Karen pulled a feather duster from her bucket of cleaning things and brandished it triumphantly at Sara, as though it were her magic wand. 'Off you go then. Sooner or later you'll meet your prince too, mark my words.'

◆ ◆ ◆

'Hello? Is there anybody there?'

Sara jumped. She hadn't been expecting anyone for at least another hour.

'Oh, I'm sorry. Did I startle you? My name's Nicola Carter. I'm Hamish and Matthew's best woman.' A tall, slender individual, dressed in flowing white linen, stood in the kitchen doorway.

Sara came to shake her hand. 'Please do come in. You're most welcome.'

'I'm staying at a rental property not far from here. Thought I'd come by before the Hibernian hordes descend on you, because I'd like to see where the ceremony's going to be on Saturday. I'm going to be conducting the proceedings – it's a huge honour, but just a bit nerve-wracking too.'

'Of course. Let me show you where I thought might be best.'

Sara led her to the viewpoint, where a wisteria-draped pergola framed the silver thread of the river in the valley below. Clusters of sweetly scented flowers hung among the lush green leaves.

'We can set chairs out here, with this as the backdrop. The timing's perfect as the wisteria's just come into its second bloom.'

'Oh, this is gorgeous!' Nicola exclaimed. 'What an amazing place. Of course, I'd expect nothing less from Matthew and Hamish. They've obviously done their research. Have you been here long?' She quizzed Sara about the château and the restoration project with interest. They wandered through the grounds and Sara showed her the main buildings – the barn, chapel and château – and the pool.

'It's wonderful. It was clever of Matthew to think of having the party out here. This way it won't be so noticeable who's here and who isn't. It's really sad, but Hamish's family would have refused to come even if it had been in Edinburgh. They just can't deal with the whole gay thing. Matthew's parents are coming, though. At least they make an effort, even if they've struggled a bit to come to terms with their son marrying a man.'

Sara felt a surge of sympathy for the pair: 'Well, I'm glad to be able to help out. You're *all* most welcome here. Now, would you like something cold to drink?' Sara glanced at her watch. 'They should be arriving any minute, so do stay – it'll be a lovely welcoming surprise for them. I can offer you wine, beer, or something non-alcoholic?'

'A glass of iced water would be great.'

Sara and Nicola settled themselves at a table on the terrace. 'So you said you're staying in the area for the summer?'

'Yes. I've rented a *gîte* over near Gensac. I thought I might as well spend a few weeks out here. I have to pop back to London every now and then for work, but it's so easy from Bergerac. It was the wedding that gave me the idea, since I'd be coming out for that anyway.'

Cars began to pull into the parking area. 'Here they are,' said Sara. 'Let's go down.'

Amid the slamming of car doors, cries of welcome rang out as the wedding party spotted Nicola. 'Darling! You got here before us. You're looking fabulous! All this wine and sunshine are obviously doing you the world of good!'

The throng were almost all as casually elegant as Nicola, beautiful people in beautiful clothes: pastel cashmere jumpers draped over shoulders (on the men) and lots of trendily crushed linen (on the women). It was easy to spot Mr and Mrs Humphreys among them, looking slightly lost in sensible, crease-proof M&S beige polyester, Mrs Humphreys' features masked under thick face powder and bright pink lipstick. As Sara introduced herself, one of the good-looking young men produced a set of bagpipes from an instrument case and began to play.

'Piped in from the very start, that's most impressive,' smiled Nicola.

'I can't tell you the trouble he had getting those on to the Ryanair flight! They charge extra for everything, even musical instruments,' Hamish exclaimed.

Summoned by the skirl of the pipes, Antoine and Héloise appeared from the direction of the piggery (Héloise's blouse buttoned up slightly skew-whiff, Sara couldn't help noticing) to help carry bags and show guests to their rooms, and the colourful, chattering procession followed the piper up to the château.

◆ ◆ ◆

The early morning air was cool and fresh, the sun just beginning to infuse the clear blue sky with the promise of heat to come. Sara was going quietly about her work in the kitchen, setting out the breakfast things, when there was a hesitant tap on the door.

'Mrs Humphreys, good morning. You've got a beautiful day for the party. Can I get you a cup of tea?'

'Oh, dear, that would be lovely.' She sat herself down at the table with a sigh.

'Are you all right?'

'Fine, thanks. Thank you, that's so kind, just a tiny splash of milk. I couldn't sleep. Too much excitement, I suppose.' She sighed again, looking older as she hadn't yet put her make-up on, and her features seemed to have sagged with a sadness that Sara couldn't help but notice. Mrs Humphreys' shoulders slumped and she pressed her fingers to her temples and then her eyes.

'Have you got a headache?' Sara asked solicitously. 'I can find you something for it if you like?'

Mrs Humphreys sat perfectly still, her head still resting in her hands as though it were too heavy for her to support. And then she said, very faintly, 'We've lost him.'

Sara came over and sat down beside her, putting a gentle hand on her arm.

'Sorry.' Mrs Humphreys pulled herself together a little, fishing a tissue out of her pocket. 'It's just . . . he's all we've got.' She spoke hesitantly. 'Matthew's our only child. We'd dreamed of grandchildren, a daughter-in-law, being part of a bigger family. But Hamish's parents won't have anything to do with us – I think they blame us for Matthew and Hamish being together. And we don't feel part of this world they're in.' She swept her arm wide, encompassing the château, the guests, the pastel cashmere and the crumpled linen.

'But you must be so proud of Matthew.' Sara patted her arm. 'He's famous! And going to be one of the top designers in the fashion world. And the two of them seem so happy together. I've seen a few couples come through here and I can tell you not all of them have looked as rock solid as Hamish and your son do.'

Mrs Humphreys blew her nose loudly and nodded slowly.

Encouraged, Sara continued, 'I know it's a very different world to the one you've known. But surely the most important thing is to support Matthew in being who he is. Having to pretend to be something you're not is one of the most lonely, isolating things there is.'

As she said this, the sudden heartfelt surge of emotion she felt was surprising; she realised that there were parallels here. There'd been times with Gavin's family – and especially his mother – when she'd felt inadequate. She'd tried to adapt to Mrs Farrell's idea of what the perfect girlfriend should be: arm candy for her precious son. In fact, now Sara came to think of it, perhaps that was when she'd first begun to feel that she was losing her voice; she'd stopped venturing an opinion when she knew she'd only be ignored, finding it easier to defer to Gavin, just as his mother did. And of course, in her own fractured family she'd quickly learned to put her own needs at the back of the queue, well behind those of her stepsiblings. No wonder she'd lost so much of her sense of self by the time Gavin left. Well, she'd learned that lesson: she was going to be true to herself from here on in. And then she found herself reflecting that some people – say, well, Thomas, for example – seemed to like her just as she was . . .

She pulled her focus firmly back to Mrs Humphreys. 'If Hamish's parents see you getting on well with both the boys, maybe they'll come round in the end. And the last thing you want is to lose touch with your son. Anyway,' Sara said robustly, 'you're going to want to be invited to be in the front row at his catwalk shows! What woman wouldn't? I shall look out for you in the pages of *Vogue* and *Harper's*.'

Mrs Humphreys managed a faint nod. 'Not to mention *Social Style* magazine,' she said, with a watery smile.

'Really?' said Sara, impressed.

'Yes, dear, didn't you know? Nicola is the editor. She's already covered some of Matthew's work. She's become a good friend of both the boys. They didn't want their wedding – or partnership, or whatever we're supposed to call it – in the magazine though. That would have been too much for Hamish's family.'

'Wow. Well, I'm extremely honoured that they chose Château Bellevue de Coulliac for their celebration. What exalted company you keep! Now, drink that tea – things always seem a little more manageable after a cuppa. And tell me, what are you wearing to the party?'

At that moment, Matthew appeared. 'Aha, I thought I heard the encouraging clink of teacups.' He put his arms around his mother and hugged her.

'Good morning, dear.' She rested her head on his shoulder for a second, her eyes closing. 'I've got a new blue dress,' she said, responding to Sara's question. 'And I did bring a fascinator with me, but I don't know if I shall wear it, it's a bit daring for me.'

'Oh, Mum, that's wonderful!' Matthew's eyes gleamed bright with what Sara suspected might just be a tear or two. 'You've gone to so much trouble – I can't tell you how much that means to me and Hamish. Of course you must wear it! You'll be the belle of the ball. I'll come and help you fix it in place when you're ready, if you like. Just like at the shows.'

Mrs Humphreys nodded. 'Thank you, my darling boy. I'd really like that.' She nodded again, and this time it seemed to Sara that she was smiling right at her. 'Thank you so much.'

Matthew turned, still with an arm around his mother. 'And Sara, we're a few women short this evening. When it comes to dancing reels, it would be a huge help if you'd join us. I know it's above and beyond your job description, but we'd love it if you could?'

'Why, thank you! I haven't danced in ages. That would be so much fun.'

◆ ◆ ◆

Sara peered into the misted depths of the mirror in the cottage's tiny bathroom. After a long day of preparations, she was hastily getting ready for the ceremony. She would usually take a quick shower and then change into her wedding 'uniform' of a smart but unobtrusive navy shirt dress, but today she had put on one of flame-coloured silk. Its fitted bodice flattered her slim figure and the fluid folds of the skirt flared just above the knee. She was trying to tell herself that she was only making the extra effort because of the guests, and the presence of the fashion world, but she couldn't quite push the image out of her mind of the man who would be playing the music at the dance tonight. She dabbed on her lip gloss and then lightly ran a finger over her lips, reminded of the brush of Thomas's fleeting, momentary kiss when they were on the weir. Had it been anything other than a passing whim in that perfect, romantic setting? The memory brought a flush to her cheeks, the glow heightened by the colour of her dress.

She brushed her long dark hair, pulling herself together, and then squared her shoulders at her reflection in the mirror, ready for work.

It was the end of a hot August afternoon and the guests, summoned once again by the sound of the pipes, were beginning to assemble at the viewpoint, elegant in their wedding finery. Conscious of the time, Sara gently encouraged them to take their seats. A welcome breath of breeze cooled her hot cheeks and made the hemline of her skirt flutter and flow.

Once everyone was seated and Nicola had taken her place under the pergola, Sara went back to the terrace where Hamish and Matthew were waiting with Mr and Mrs Humphreys. Matthew was making the final adjustments to his mother's headpiece, a flourish of blue-and-cream feathers that sat jauntily in her hair. He hugged her close. 'There. You look wonderful. I'm so proud to have such a chic mother.'

She held him at arm's length, taking in the elegant cut of his suit and minutely adjusting the deep-red rose in his jacket button-hole. 'And we couldn't be prouder of you. Both of you.' She turned to embrace Hamish, resplendent in his kilt. 'We're so happy that you're making this commitment to each other, and we wish you much joy.'

Mr Humphreys cleared his throat, looking less at ease than the other three. But, after a moment's hesitation, he hugged each of the boys in turn, awkwardly clapping them on the back, man-style, in a display of affection that seemed really most unlike him.

Matthew turned to Sara. 'And look at you! You do scrub up well, Miss Audrey-Hepburn-Cheekbones.'

She blushed and smiled. 'Thank you. Are we ready to go?'

The others nodded and so she led Mr and Mrs Humphreys to their seats, the signal for the piper to strike up 'Highland Cathedral'. To a round of applause, Hamish and Matthew walked hand in hand up the aisle between the chairs to where Nicola waited, smiling.

After the short, but moving, ceremony and the couple's exchange of their heartfelt vows, the piper led the way back to the courtyard where the caterers were waiting with flutes of champagne and trays of canapés. Their friends snapped away with cameras and phones, exclaiming at the picturesque backdrop of the ancient stonework and soft drifts of flowers.

Aperitifs over, Sara and Hélène began to usher people into the marquee. On this warm evening, the sides had been rolled back to allow the breeze through, the garden setting enhancing the arrangements of deep-red roses and hazy fronds of asparagus fern that had been used to decorate the dining tent.

After Hélène had departed, Sara left the caterers in charge while the meal ran its course. She slipped back to the château kitchen for a welcome few moments when she could sit down and grab her own supper. The caterers had made up three extra plates of food and Sara pulled up a chair at the table where Antoine and Thomas were already tucking in.

Thomas gave a low whistle when he saw her. 'Wow, Boss. Looking good tonight.'

'Why, thank you, Monsieur DJ. I'm looking forward to your reels. Antoine, we'd better bring a few more bottles of whisky up from the cellar. These Scots will probably get through quite a bit later on.' She reminded herself that she was still on duty, even if she was mixing business with pleasure for once.

When they could hear the sound of applause for the last of the speeches, the three of them crossed the courtyard to the barn, each carrying a couple of bottles of a single malt. Setting these on the bar, Thomas took his place behind the decks and flicked the switches for the lights. Above their heads, the glitter ball began to revolve, spangling their bodies with its white diamonds.

The strains of the first dance rang out. Hamish and Matthew were leading off with the Gay Gordons, to the delight of their friends whose cool elegance was beginning to give way to more animated whoops and whistles.

The caller announced Strip the Willow: 'Sets of eight, please, boys down one side, girls down the other, or just choose whichever one you'd like to be!'

Mr Humphreys was propping up the bar, deep in conversation with Antoine about the range of whiskies on offer and the relative merits of an eighteen-year-old Bunnahabhain versus a twelve-year-old Cardhu. Matthew grabbed his mother's hand, and Hamish caught Nicola, pulling her on to the dance floor. The piper materialised at Sara's elbow. 'Ya dancin'?' he asked.

'If you're asking,' she replied with a smile.

The caller was skilled at his job, walking them through the dance first, before giving Thomas the nod to set the music playing. Matthew twirled his mother down the set and then took his turn back up again and, by the time they were both spinning back down together, Mrs Humphreys' fascinator had assumed a distinctly rakish angle, and she was flushed and laughing giddily.

Sara's feet flew when it came to her turn, her red dress swirling as her partner spun her deftly. Once they'd reached their places at the bottom of the line again, she glanced over at Thomas. He was watching the dancers with a broad smile, clapping his hands and stamping his feet in time with the rest of them. His eyes met hers in the dizzying disco lights and she grinned back as he let out a whoop as wild as that of any of the Scots. Flinging her head back, Sara laughed with the sheer joyous exhilaration of the dance.

◆　◆　◆

She'd slipped away some time after midnight, as the mood of the party began to mellow, the music slowing. It was much later than she normally would have stayed but she'd been having so much fun she'd hardly noticed the time. Her head was still buzzing and she didn't feel the slightest bit tired, so she sat down in a deckchair on the terrace outside the cottage door, kicking off her shoes and propping her feet on the low wall in front of her. The sky was amazing tonight, a velvety black, copiously sprinkled with millions of winking stars. The Milky Way was a sheer veil, draping itself above her. She was reminded of the veil of water on the weir, on that magical walk across the river with Thomas. She rested her head against the chair back, gazing upwards, remembering.

In the barn, the music fell silent. She listened to the calls of 'goodnight' as the guests meandered back to their rooms and their cars.

Suddenly, she was aware that he was standing there before her. He held up a champagne bottle and two glasses. 'I wondered if you might still be awake. It seemed a shame to waste this last half-bottle. In fact, as a winemaker myself, I know how very disappointed Louis Roederer would be if it was not drunk on this most perfect of nights.'

She smiled up at him. 'Well, in that case, I certainly wouldn't want to upset your good friend Louis.'

Thomas poured the champagne and handed her a glass, sitting down in the deckchair next to hers. She took a sip, the bubbles as delicately heady as distilled starlight, and gave a little sigh of happiness.

Watching her in the darkness, a slow smile lit up Thomas's face.

'What?'

'I was just reflecting on something my English teacher told me,' he mused.

'What's that?'

'Apparently there are about twice as many words in the English language as there are in French. But in spite of this, we French have many more phrases for expressing joy than the English do. Maybe that says something about our different cultures.'

She pondered this for a moment. 'What made you think of that?'

He shrugged. 'This evening. The party. Seeing those people dancing together. Watching you dance. Being here with you now. You embody a phrase we have in French: *joie de vivre*. You know it?'

She nodded. 'Yes. We cold-hearted English even borrow it ourselves sometimes. I suppose it means, literally, something like *the joy of being alive*? "Exuberance" would probably be our closest word.'

'I think it's more than that really. It's the very essence of life. Without joy, life is empty.' He looked about him, taking in the dark outline of the château, the black velvet of the lawn spreading out at their feet like a deep pool, bordered on the far side by the faint glow of white roses, the silk of their petals picked out in the moonlight. 'You've created a place of joy here, Sara. It's a place so filled with beauty and love that it allows people to find their true *joie de vivre*.'

She raised her glass to him, smiling back, quietly pleased that he felt the same way she did and understood the place so well. Then she tilted her face to the night sky once more.

Thomas sat beside her in companionable silence, gazing upwards too.

Sara gasped: 'Oh, look! A shooting star! And another!'

As they watched, the sky became alive with movement suddenly and then it was gone again as quickly as it had come.

'*Les larmes de Saint Laurent.* Saint Laurence's tears. It's a meteor shower,' said Thomas. 'They come each year at this time. It's dust from the tail of a comet, showering down on us and burning up in the Earth's atmosphere.'

'There's another one!' she pointed.

He turned to look at her enraptured profile as she scanned the sky for more.

'You must make a wish,' he smiled.

She turned to meet his gaze, her eyes dark. 'What would your wish be, Thomas?'

'Oh, let me see. I think my wish would be to sit under a star-filled sky, sipping fine champagne with a beautiful girl in a red dress, whose smile is as bright as the starlight itself.' He blinked slowly. 'Wow, look at that! These shooting-star wishes really do come true,' he smiled. 'And what would yours be, Sara?'

She held his gaze for a long moment. And then reached out her hand and brushed the side of his face with her fingertips. Getting to her feet, she set down her glass and held out a hand to him. And, without a word, the two of them went into the cottage, shutting the door quietly behind them, as the night sky lit up once again in a shower of stardust.

◆ ◆ ◆

Sara hummed a Scottish reel under her breath, as she and Karen dried glasses following the Sunday brunch. It was a mellow afternoon, and the guests were lingering over their coffees on the terrace. Sara had noticed Mr and Mrs Humphreys looking relaxed and happy as they chatted with Nicola Carter, who was regaling them with titbits of gossip from the world of glossy magazines. Sara smiled to herself.

Karen nudged her in the ribs. 'Someone's in an awfully good mood today.'

'Just enjoying the fact that this wedding's been a good example of what such occasions really should be: a bonding experience all round and a gesture of support and solidarity for the couple making the commitment. It seems obvious, but it's funny how many events we've had here that have felt more like a tug of war between the two families, or a competition to see which can put the other side down more.'

Sara imagined, just for a moment, what her and Gavin's wedding might have been like, with her own mother and father, long divorced, still hardly on speaking terms, each with their own new partner and assorted stepchildren with whom she had little in common; and then the added dimension of Mrs Farrell, stirring the pot at every opportunity with a snooty put-down or a superior look. Thank goodness she didn't have to go through with such an ordeal now. She felt the last shreds of self-pity wash away in a wave of relief.

'Hmm,' responded Karen. 'And speaking of bonding experiences, it sounds as if you've been pretty busy on that front yourself. Is there anything you'd like to tell me?'

Sara paused, still clutching her damp tea towel, her hands on her hips. 'What on *earth* have you heard? Honestly, the gossip around this place is truly outrageous!'

Karen carried on slotting wine glasses back into the honeycomb cells of the storage crate, nonchalant.

'Well, when I popped into the bakery this morning, Madame Fournier told me that I'd just missed Thomas Cortini, who'd apparently been doing the Sunday morning croissant run for Château Bellevue in place of Mademoiselle Sara. She couldn't help noticing that he was wearing his smart shirt and pants, such as might be worn when DJ-ing a wedding party the night before. And apparently he'd been in an extremely good mood, whistling a Scottish tune, not unlike the one you've just been humming to yourself this fine morning, Snow White.'

'And so she put two and two together and made five?' retorted Sara.

'No, but she did put one and one together and make two. But don't worry – I cunningly threw her off the scent by telling her he must have spent the night with one of the wedding guests. And, given that it hasn't escaped the notice of the good people of Coulliac that this particular function has an especially gay air about it, that's given Madame Fournier a *great* deal to think about!'

Sara buried her face in the tea towel. 'Oh, Karen, you didn't?'

'Of course, I *could* scotch these rumours by going back and telling her that I'd got it wrong and that I have a categorical admission that he was with a certain girl up here instead . . .'

Sara hesitated, coming out from behind the tea towel, blushing. 'All right. I admit it.'

'Gotcha! I knew it,' Karen crowed. 'Oh, and by the way, Madame Fournier already did too. Only a rookie gossipmonger would have believed anything otherwise, and she's a world expert.'

Grinning smugly, Karen carried on putting away the glasses.

Sara was relieved to turn back to her task, polishing each wine glass with deliberate concentration. She knew she ought to be regretting last night. After all, she'd sworn off men for life (so much for willpower, then) and it was probably a big mistake to get involved with someone she worked with. And she blushed to think how quickly it had happened after Gavin's departure. But who could have resisted the starlight and the champagne, such a perfect setting . . . such a man. She put it down to his irresistible *joie de vivre*, the life force he'd brought to the two weddings he'd participated in so far . . . the way the sun came out whenever he walked into the room. But there was more to him too, she knew now. His confiding in her the other day had made her feel so much closer to him. *Careful now*, she admonished herself. *You're not going to fall for him; you know he'll only leave you and break your heart.* It had been a temporary lapse, that was all. A fling as a result of a glass of champagne too many and all those months of loneliness and frustration. It had felt so good to lie in someone's arms again, to feel wanted. Maybe even – although she hardly dared think the thought – to feel loved . . .

Just then, Nicola Carter appeared in the kitchen. 'Sara, I'm heading back to the *gîte* now. Just wanted to thank you all for making it such a perfect celebration for the boys. We've all had a wonderful time.'

'Oh, can you hang on a sec? I wondered whether you'd like to take some of the flowers from the marquee back with you to brighten up your holiday house. Matthew said they don't want them – after all, they can hardly take them back on the plane.' Sara wrapped an armful of the roses in damp newspaper and covered it with a plastic bag.

'Beautiful, I'd love them – thanks.' Nicola fished in her bag and handed Sara her business card. 'Here's my mobile number and email address. Keep in touch. And let me know if I can ever be of help. We might even include Château Bellevue de Coulliac in a feature in *Social Style* magazine one of these days.'

Chapter 6

Patti & Thorne

Patti &
Thorne

tie the knot

On Saturday 18 August
At Château Bellevue de Coulliac

From 4.00 p.m.

RSVP: admin@sharpe–productions.com

It was not unusual for the bright yellow post van to call at Château Bellevue de Coulliac. As far as possible, Sara bought supplies locally to support the region's shopkeepers, but for some of the more exotic requests – heart-shaped helium balloons, for example, and biodegradable delphinium-petal confetti; personalised fortune cookies and glitter-butterfly table decorations – she ordered online from specialist suppliers, resulting in frequent visits by the *facteur* to deliver an intriguing array of cardboard boxes. The postman liked nothing better than to stand and chat for a few minutes, gleaning all sorts of fascinating snippets about the latest bizarre new ways *les Anglo-Saxons* had come up with for celebrating their nuptials. But today there were no boxes to drop off, just a solitary registered-delivery envelope. As she signed for it, Sara was careful to give nothing away, smiling and chatting with the postman while the envelope, with her name and address on it in Gavin's handwriting, glowed radioactively in her hand.

'There's a rumour that next weekend there's going to be a rock concert at Château Bellevue. Is it really true that The Steel Thornes are coming?'

The Steel Thornes hadn't had a hit record for about a decade, but they still toured, belting out their heavy-metal back catalogue at the lesser venues across Europe. They had an enthusiastic fan base on the Continent, even if the audiences at their gigs were generally a sea of balding heads and bulging paunches nowadays.

Sara confirmed that this was, in fact, the case. She'd managed pretty well to keep a lid on it that ageing rock legend Thorne Sharpe and his long-term girlfriend Patti Monahan had booked the château for the coming weekend. But she'd had to go and speak to Monsieur le Maire about security (the two rather sleepy local *gendarmes* had been notified accordingly) and to request permission for the sound-and-light show that was planned for the after-party, so it was inevitable that the news would seep out.

'I hope it's not going to upset people in Coulliac. We're far enough from our nearest neighbours that it shouldn't be *too* loud, and they've promised that the live music will finish by eleven p.m.'

'Oh no, not at all,' the postman assured her. 'In fact, the Café de la Paix is putting out extra chairs. The whole village is intending to come and watch from the square – I just hope it's going to be loud *enough*. It's not every day we have a real live rock band come to Coulliac! People are coming from far and wide – if the mayor could get away with selling tickets for it, he would.'

Once she'd wished the postman a *bonne journée*, Sara made herself walk back inside and sit down at the table before tearing open the envelope. As she read, the hand holding the sheet of paper began to tremble.

The tone of the letter was cool, and some of the phrases were couched in legalese, which made Sara suspect Gavin had already sought professional advice. Either that or he was trying to scare her into submission. Either way, she was shocked that he was resorting to bullying her like this. The bottom line was that he wanted his money out. He wanted sixty per cent of the profits from this season's earnings, in line with his shareholding in the business, and he wanted the château put on the market straight away, in the hope of selling it by the end of the year so that he could get his investment back.

Of course he was entitled to a fair share of the profits; Sara would never have dreamed of withholding anything that was due to him. But she was doing all the work now. He also knew full well that more investment in the property was needed if the business was to be a viable proposition in future years. They'd gone through the figures together at the outset and had agreed to plough this year's profits back in. There were still several major projects in the pipeline – her plans for the garden, a new roof needed on the stable block, the rewiring of the barn – not to mention the replastering of the wall in the cottage and the general maintenance that these old buildings constantly demanded.

Sara read and reread the words on the page, as though their meaning might change if she did, hoping for a glimmer of empathy from the man with whom she'd shared three years of her life. But there was none. He knew exactly what he was doing. His demands sounded the death knell for any hopes she might have had for staying at Château Bellevue.

She pressed her fingers to her throbbing temples, trying to think straight. She'd need to take some advice herself. She had no idea what the legal position would be here in France and she'd have to speak to the bank manager and the accountant, and then an estate agent most probably.

It would be a terrible time to sell. She was well aware that property prices had fallen further since they'd bought the château. They stood to lose money. Her more meagre share would be eaten away significantly, leaving her to limp back to England without even enough to relaunch her landscape gardening business in London, let alone afford to live there. Unlike Gavin, she had no family home to go back to. It was a disaster.

She raised her head and gazed out of the window to the garden beyond, where clouds of white gaura nodded gracefully beneath the silver leaves of an olive tree. And suddenly she was overcome by a surge of protectiveness, so fierce that it charged her body with a visceral strength.

She belonged here. It was more than a thought; it was a certain knowledge. She thought of the ledger recording the weddings from the past, of how much she wanted to be the one to continue that history. She'd never really felt she'd belonged anywhere before now. But this was *her* time to be in *this* place. For the first time in her life, she'd begun to put down roots, anchoring herself to this limestone ridge as surely as the château itself was anchored here. She had a vision of the finished garden that she wanted to create here, so vivid that it already felt real. She couldn't let Gavin destroy her with his cruelly casual selfishness. She had to find a way to stay.

Thomas appeared in the doorway, whistling cheerfully. He'd gone to make sure everything was all right back at the vineyard that morning, to open the mail and check whether any new orders had come in, but now he was back. 'It may be a difficult year for the vines, but at least the tomatoes are thriving,' he said, setting down a basket of sun-warmed vegetables from the *potager* at Château de la Chapelle.

Sara folded the letter and stuck it in her apron pocket, turning her face up to meet his as he stooped to kiss her. She wasn't about to involve him in her troubles, but she was thankful for the reassurance of his smile, in which nothing was written but pure joy at seeing her again.

◆ ◆ ◆

'*Oh, mon Dieu!* I can't believe you didn't tell me before now!' Thomas had just read the programme for the coming weekend. 'You mean to tell me I'm going to be the DJ at the wedding of Thorne Sharpe? That's like playing for royalty!'

'You clearly don't listen to enough gossip, Tommy-boy,' laughed Karen. 'It's common knowledge on the street in Coulliac.'

'Well, I was *trying* to be discreet,' Sara smiled. 'His production company asked us to keep it hush-hush. My guess is they've sold the rights to one of the gossip magazines and so they don't want any other media staking out the château. Anyway, there won't be too much for you to do. The band's playing until eleven at the latest and they only want the disco for about an hour after that. There's a truckload of roadies arriving on Friday with the sound system for the band and the light show. The guests will only be arriving on

Saturday morning and most are leaving on Sunday. So it's a short, sharp one this time.'

Thomas sped off excitedly to the barn to prepare some new playlists in honour of The Steel Thornes. 'They've requested a mixture of dance music,' Sara called after him. 'It's a disco, remember! They'll probably have had enough heavy metal once the band's done their stint.'

Sara immersed herself briskly in the physical exertion that the changeover entailed, thankful for the distraction, and for having the rest of the team there, so excited at the coming celebrity-filled weekend and their own role in it: it helped to take her mind off Gavin's letter, burning a hole in her apron pocket. She couldn't afford to be distracted by it. This wedding was high-profile, no matter how discreet an affair they tried to make it, and it would be a massive boost to the business, as long as everything went perfectly to plan: the pressure was well and truly on.

'Blimey, someone's had their Vegemite this morning,' Karen observed when she found Sara scrubbing the bath in the honeymoon suite with cathartic vigour, working off some of her anxious tension.

It wasn't just this wedding. Try as she might to focus on the business at hand, the uncertainty over her future here was a constant worry in the back of her mind. Her phone call to the bank yesterday afternoon had been fruitless, the unanswered ringtone echoing in her ear until she had realised that, of course, it was closed on Mondays. She'd have no time to call today, and, in any case, she didn't want to do it while the others were around. She'd decided it would probably be better to go down in person tomorrow; she should have time, as long as they broke the back of the preparations today.

By Friday morning, excitement crackled in the air as the truck rumbled up the driveway and manoeuvred to get as close to the barn as possible. The two hefty roadies jumped down from the cab, introducing themselves simply as Stan and Andy, and began unloading flight cases full of kit.

Sara was amused to note that, while they weren't officially on duty today, the whole team just happened to have turned up, drawn by the lure of Château Bellevue's first ever rock concert-cum-wedding: they'd all be there tomorrow as well, the opportunity to have ringside seats at a celeb-spangled party – and the kudos this assured within the local community – too exciting to miss. Karen's husband, Didier, a lifelong Steel Thornes fan, was also coming, and Karen had reported that he'd even dug out an old denim jacket with the band's logo on it, which fitted fine – just as long as he didn't actually try to button it up over his age-thickened midriff.

Thomas was buzzing with his role in it all and he was on hand today to help with the set-up. Over a lunch of bread and cheese, washed down with several bottles of beer, the roadies regaled them with stories of life on the road with the band.

'Where was it we did that concert in the old Mig hangar?' Stan prompted Andy, drawing hard on his cigarette.

'Kazakhstan, wasn't it? Or – no, Poland, I think. Was it after Berlin or before?'

'Dunno. It all blurs into one when you're on tour. We're in a different venue every night and sleeping on the tour bus on the way to the next concert most days. 'Course, usually it wouldn't be us driving the truck, let alone setting up the kit. But we've been with the band for ten years now; we'd do anything for them. They're like family really. It's such a small party this time, so we agreed to do it. Thorne insisted on keeping it that way, didn't want it to be a full-on gig like his label would've liked. It *is* supposed to be him an' Patti's wedding after all. And if the rumours are true and she really is, you know' – Stan's hand described an even more rounded belly in front of his already generous girth – 'then it's not surprising.'

Around the table, they all digested this juicy nugget of gossip and Sara hoped against hope that it wouldn't be in general circulation on the streets of Coulliac within the hour.

'So how many trucks would you normally have on tour?' Thomas hung on the roadies' every word, enthralled.

''Bout a dozen normally. Maybe a few less for festivals. We've just brought the bare essentials for tomorrow, yeah? Speakers, amps, a basic lighting rig, sound desk, lighting desk. Some staging. Drum kit. One laser.'

'A laser! Where's that going?'

'It's a SkyTracker. It'll be beaming into the sky above the château. Production assistant's checked with air traffic control so it won't interfere with any aircraft. She said she was sorting out a gennie from the local hire place – have they delivered it yet? And the pyro guy's turning up this afternoon, yeah?' Andy checked with Sara.

'If a "gennie" is a generator then yes, that's here. And if "pyro" means fireworks, then yes to that as well: we've got a local specialist coming – he should be here at two.'

'Okay, we'll need to co-ordinate with him. Does he speak English?'

'I'll translate for you,' Thomas volunteered eagerly.

As Sara cleared away the lunch things, she watched Thomas through the kitchen window where he was helping run lengths of cable from the barn to the generator that would provide the power for the show.

They'd spent every night together since that first starlit evening last weekend, and it felt so natural being with him. She hadn't thought at all about where their relationship might be going; it was a novelty simply enjoying their easy lovemaking in the tiny cottage up on their hilltop fortress, tucked away from the rest of the world. It felt like time out of time.

But even when she was with him, she was quietly carrying the heavy burden of her anxiety about the future on her shoulders. It felt like a physical weight, exhausting to sustain. She sat down and rested her head for a moment, cushioning it on her arms on the scrubbed wooden surface of the kitchen table. She was beginning to suspect that Fate, cunningly disguised as the French banking system, was conspiring against her. She'd turned up at the bank on Wednesday, only to find that – of course! – it was a public holiday. And when she'd phoned the next day she'd been told that, *non*, the manager was, in fact, away on holiday and wouldn't be back for another ten days. And *non*, she couldn't make an appointment with anyone else. And *non*, they couldn't put an appointment in his diary; it would have to wait for his return. An email address? *Non*. So, if his colleagues were anything to go by, she had a nasty feeling she knew what the bank manager was going to say in response to her request for a loan to buy out Gavin's share of the business.

Faced with the unhelpful brick wall of French bureaucracy on top of Gavin's desertion, she was starting to feel she might be losing the will to fight, the surge of fierce possessiveness for the château, which had swept through her veins so strongly a few days ago, dissolving now in the cold light of financial reality. Niggling doubts were creeping in, especially when, alone in the cottage, she reread Gavin's officious letter. Perhaps, after all, the best thing really would be to sell, cutting her losses and leaving. She wouldn't want to stay anywhere else in the area, with Thomas gone and her beloved château gazing down reproachfully at her from its hilltop perch. She knew that soon she'd have to call the agent who'd sold them the château and ask him to put it back on the market.

So would she still be here in a few months' time? And would Thomas already have set off on his travels? Was that what he really wanted from life? Watching him at lunch, caught up in tales of life as a roadie, she could see he was already imagining himself there, footloose and fancy-free, new horizons luring him away.

She was resigned to this being just a fling. And in any case, she told herself, that was all she wanted right now. After Gavin's humiliating betrayal and departure, she wasn't sure she could ever really trust anyone again. There were still wounds that needed to heal, even if time spent with Thomas did feel like the perfect balm for her bruised and battered soul. And now it occurred to her that maybe the reason it was so good was precisely that there was no future. Perhaps short-term, no-strings affairs were all she would be capable of committing to from here on in. Next year – and no doubt a return to celibacy – would come round soon enough, so she'd better make the most of this miraculous, joyful, warm-hearted man while he was here. No need to protect her heart, just live for the moment and enjoy it while it lasted.

Karen and the girls were helping wash up and put away when Thomas came through the kitchen, on the way to tracking down a screwdriver. On his way past, he caught her in his arms and kissed her full on the lips, making no attempt whatsoever to keep up any pretence of discretion in front of the others. Karen laughed as the Héls Belles exchanged a knowing nod of approval.

And then Thomas came back through, screwdriver in hand, and did it again, hamming it up for the benefit of the others, almost sweeping Sara off her feet as he bent her backwards in a tango hold. Righting her again, he grinned and said, 'Come on, guys, Andy and Stan are setting up the drum kit – who wants a go?'

'I'll be along in a minute.' Sara chivvied the others out of the kitchen, suddenly needing a moment to herself, overwhelmed by the extremes of emotion that swept through her.

From the barn, she heard a gust of laughter and then the rhythmic beat of a drum. She pulled herself together, squaring her shoulders, and, taking a deep breath, went to rejoin the others.

◆　◆　◆

Sara was helping the harried-looking girl from the production company allocate bedrooms. 'Thorne and Patti are in the honeymoon suite, of course. Then I thought Mr Black might like the garden room as it's the next biggest.' Richie Black managed The Steel Thornes and Sara was conscious that his status as owner of The Black Label meant he expected to take precedence over the other members of the band. The girl checked a list on her clipboard and made a couple of notes. She'd arrived before the others on a scheduled flight that morning; the main party was arriving by private plane, and a small fleet of Mercedes minibuses had been hired to bring them to the château. 'Okay. Thanks, Sara, it's all looking good.'

Some of the guests – the bass guitarist and drummer, an up-and-coming rapper who was also signed to The Black Label, a couple of former supermodels – weren't even going to be staying the night. They'd drop in for the party and then be driven back to the airport, where their respective executive jets would whisk them off to their next exotic destination for work or play. 'How the other half live,' Karen had remarked, as Sara was running through the arrangements at the pre-wedding briefing session.

◆　◆　◆

'I can't believe how down-to-earth they are!' Hélène said as she was helping Sara prepare a tray of tea things to take to Patti and Thorne, now safely installed in the honeymoon suite.

'I know,' Sara smiled. 'It's not exactly rock'n'roll, is it? A pot of Earl Grey tea and a plate of shortbread.'

Patti had looked grey with tiredness when they arrived, and Thorne had put a protective arm around her shoulders. He'd turned down Richie Black's invitation to join the others for a couple of jugs of margaritas by the pool: 'Nah, think we'll just chill for a while.'

Antoine was in his element, mixing cocktails with a flourish, with an admiring Héloise at his side squeezing limes and trotting back to the cellar for bottles of tequila when needed.

Sara tapped gently on the door of the honeymoon suite. 'Come in!' Thorne called.

She set the tray down and Patti emerged from the direction of the bathroom, smiling gratefully at the sight of the home-made biscuits. 'Oh, great.' She took one. 'This might help settle my stomach.' She stroked her faintly rounded belly, a gentle curve on her tall, skinny frame. 'Four months in and the morning sickness is still as bad as it was at the start.' She shook her head ruefully.

'Come and lie down for a while.' Thorne was solicitous. 'Gotta save your energy for your wedding, doll.'

Patti lowered herself thankfully on to the bed.

'Is there anything else I can bring you?' Sara asked.

'Don't suppose you've got any Rennies, have you?' Patti asked with a sigh. 'I know it doesn't exactly go with the image Richie wants us to project, but after the flight I've got terrible heartburn.'

Sara laughed. 'Of course. Coming right up!'

'Thanks, you're a star. And thanks for having us in your lovely château. It's a stunning spot you've got here. We were determined to find the kind of place that *we* wanted for the wedding. If it'd been left up to Richie, he'd have had us getting married on a superyacht in St Tropez, or some flash resort in the Caribbean.'

'Yeah, or Vegas, baby! That was his other suggestion – do it on stage at the end of the show.' Thorne shook his head, his trademark shoulder-length dark hair shot with threads of silver these days. It was a look he carried off well, Sara thought. In fact, if anything, he was better-looking than ever. And Patti was still amazing, even if her model looks had softened slightly with age and pregnancy. They certainly had something, these celebrities, an aura that set them apart.

'For once, Thorne put his foot down though.' Patti smiled up at him and gently stroked his chiselled jawline as he stooped to hand her a cup of tea. 'Relaunching The Steel Thornes is one thing, but using our wedding as a PR opportunity is a step too far.'

'Yeah, be nice *not* to have the media circus for once. Today's about you and me, Patti-pan, not the band.' He laid a hand carefully on her belly. 'And the kid, of course.'

Sara was touched at having witnessed this intimate scene. She was pleased they'd chosen the château, out of all the other venues they could have had at their disposal. She wondered whether she would ever have what Patti and Thorne did – not the material wealth, and certainly not the celebrity status, but the quiet, calm warmth of intimacy and understanding that forged such a solid bond between them. Maybe even someone she could start a family of her own with . . .

She swallowed the lump in her throat. 'I'll be right back with the Rennies for you,' she said, as she reached to draw the door closed, giving them their privacy. 'Let me know if there's anything else you need.'

◆ ◆ ◆

Henri Dupont hardly knew which way to point his camera as the bevy of glitterati milled about outside the chapel. Thorne and Patti had been specific in their instructions, relayed to Sara via the production assistant at The Black Label: they wanted photos to be taken immediately before and after the service – no video though, and no photographers present at the meal and the party. So Thomas was keeping a close eye on Henri and would make sure he left once the official wedding pictures were in the can. With so much nubile celebrity temptation around, Henri was going to be loath to tear himself away.

The early evening air was heavy and humid and the champagne was flowing freely, although Sara noticed that Patti and Thorne hardly touched their glasses as they circulated among their guests before dinner. The Thornes' lead guitarist had set up an amp at the entrance to the marquee and played the bride and groom in with a rendition of the band's hit 'Perfection'.

Once everyone was safely seated, Sara popped across to the barn to make sure all was ready. Thomas was helping the two roadies with something on the panel of high-tech kit that they'd set up alongside the disco. Stan scratched his head. 'Bloody dodgy French wiring. I just hope that gennie's going to be up to the job. If we don't balance the phases right, the whole lot will blow. There! That's it. Yes! Sorted!' Stan clapped Thomas on the back as the video projector lit up the far wall. 'Guy's a natural,' he said to Sara with a grin. 'Any time you want a job on the tour, just let us know, Thomas.'

Thomas beamed. 'I may well take you up on that.'

Sara suppressed a pang of sadness, and her throat tightened at the thought of him being gone. Their paths were going to lead them in different directions soon enough, and she should be glad for him when it happened, but she knew, suddenly, that it was going to be much harder than she had ever imagined when the time came. Smiling brightly to camouflage her emotions, she moved on quickly. Everything was fine here; he didn't need her.

When dinner was over, the guests meandered across to the barn, picking their way along paths where night-scented stocks breathed their sweet perfume on to the night air.

The generator was humming in a corner behind the barn and Andy flicked a switch. Suddenly the white beam of the laser swept the sky and a faint cheer could be heard from the valley below, where the lights of the village twinkled brightly. There was a buzz from the speakers and then the band blasted into 'Heart of Steel', the hit that had launched them on to the music scene two decades earlier. As The Steel Thornes rocked Château Bellevue on its foundations, a spectacular firework display lit up the night sky.

Thomas materialised beside Sara as she stood in the shadows just beyond the open doors of the barn. He put an arm around her and pulled her to him. His eyes were alive with the thrill of the concert. He bent his mouth to her ear to make himself heard. 'Incredible! Look what you've achieved, bringing such an event to this corner of the world. It's crazy!'

She smiled up at him. 'With a lot of help from my friends.'

Another rocket exploded in the sky above their heads, the *boom* reverberating through their bodies in counterpoint to the pounding of the drums and bass guitar.

A pall of smoke hung in the air above them, the beam of the laser slicing into it. The smell of gunpowder mingled with faint undertones of cigarettes and expensive perfume that floated on the air.

Thomas glanced skywards and nudged Sara. 'It's clouded over. I hope the rain holds off until the show's over.' She nodded.

They stood together watching as the band played on. Finally, Thorne Sharpe, microphone in hand, stepped to the front of the stage. He held up his hands to quieten the cheers from the assembled wedding guests. 'Before our final number, I have an announcement to make. In case you didn't know already, my wife and I' – he paused to let the resurgence of cheers die down once again – 'are expecting a baby in February, on Valentine's Day to be precise. So this tour will be my last, for a while at least. The boys and I' – he threw out an arm to include the band – 'want to get back into the studio and record some new stuff. But in these uncertain times, the powers that be aren't convinced there's a market for The Steel Thornes' music any more. So it's going to be a question of *watch this space* . . . Who knows where we'll all be by the end of the year.'

You and me both, thought Sara in the shadows.

Lightning flickered, illuminating the scene for a second, and a growl of thunder reverberated like a soft drum roll.

'But tonight, all that matters is one thing,' Thorne continued. 'Patti: this one's for you.'

And with that, the band crashed into the opening bars of 'Perfection'. But the opening bars were as far as they got because, just as Thorne stepped to the mic to sing, there was an almighty crack and a flash of white light and then a stunned silence as the barn was plunged into darkness. From across the valley, the faint sound of cheering could be heard again as the people of Coulliac applauded this grand finale, as if The Steele Thornes had conjured up the thunderclap themselves.

Inside the barn, one or two people giggled nervously, but then a faint ripple of panic began to spread among some of the guests of a more nervous – or perhaps a more chemically enhanced – disposition.

Thinking fast, Sara stepped into the doorway. 'Sorry about this, folks – we thought we'd organised everything, but the occasional act of God is out of our control. Please stay where you are for the moment. If you have a phone on you, then a little light would be very helpful, just to keep everyone safe. Give us five minutes and we'll get the party back on track.'

Antoine, at his station behind the bar, propped his phone against an ice bucket, and Stan and Andy appeared with torches. 'That lightning strike's knocked out the gennie completely. We tried the mains lights, but it must have blown the fuse board too.'

Sara beckoned to them. 'I'll show you where it is. Thomas, can you take Karen, Didier and Hélène to the marquee and bring back as many candles as you can lay your hands on?'

The fuse board for the barn – which was fortunately on a separate circuit to the main house – was a sorry sight, with every fuse fried. Stan sucked his teeth, shaking his head.

'It's an old-style French board,' Sara explained. 'The rewiring is in the budget for next year, and you can see why! We'll need to physically replace the fuses. I've got some, but not enough for every single one. We'll have to prioritise; if we can just get the sound and lights for the disco back, we'll be okay.'

Thomas materialised at her elbow. 'Let me take over here, Sara. Don't worry, we'll work it out between us. You go and manage your guests.' She smiled at him in gratitude in the torchlight and sped back to the barn.

The atmosphere was calmer. Many of the guests had congregated at the bar, where Antoine and Héloise were doing a roaring trade by the light of several candles. Hélène, Karen and Didier (thrilled to be an official part of the proceedings now) were setting out dozens of tea lights around the walls of the barn and slowly the mellow stone began to glow with a soft light.

Sara went over to where Thorne and Patti stood near the stage. 'I'm sorry about this. But we'll have the disco up and running shortly. It's just going to take them a few minutes to change the fuses.'

'Don't worry, Sara. In fact, we quite like it like this,' smiled Patti. 'It's much more romantic this way – makes a nice change from the usual high-tech razzmatazz.'

'Yeah, it's cool.' Thorne kissed Patti lightly on the forehead. 'In fact, I'm feeling inspired. Stay right there!'

He seized a guitar that was propped against one of the now redundant amps and pulled out the lead. Drawing up a stool, he clapped his hands to get the attention of the rest of the guests.

'Since we're going back to the old way of lighting, we might as well do the same with the sound. Now, where was I before I was so rudely interrupted? Oh, yeah. Like I was saying, Patti: this one's for you.'

In the flickering light of a hundred candles, the room fell silent as he began to play.

'Thought perfection was impossible,
Until I saw you . . .'

His voice, without the microphone, was like rough velvet. He'd slowed the song down, and the poignancy of the acoustic accompaniment brought new resonance to the lyrics. He held the crowd in the palm of his hand, spellbound. But it was as if he and Patti were the only two there, and he was speaking the words of love directly to her and their unborn child.

As the last notes died away, every person there held their breath, captivated, not wanting to break the spell.

And then the room erupted in ecstatic applause.

Thomas, who had crept in halfway through the song, gave Sara a thumbs up and then hurried to his place behind the decks. Sara crossed her fingers as he switched on the kit but, thankfully, the new fuses held and the disco lights began to revolve as the music started.

Sara relaxed and turned to grin at Karen and Didier. 'Never a dull moment at Château Bellevue! Thanks, guys, you helped save the day.'

'*Incroyable.*' Didier shook his head. 'That acoustic version was amazing. I never thought that The Steel Thornes would be capable of moving me to tears.' He hugged Karen to his side.

'Get away with you, you soppy old bugger!' she laughed, but not before Sara noticed how tenderly she hugged him in return.

Love really is in the air in this magical place, she thought. But then she had to turn away as she felt a pang of loneliness. She felt like a kid with her nose pressed against a sweetshop window, looking in from the outside at something she couldn't have. It seemed to come so easily to others, finding the right person, being with them. Her heart ached with a sudden longing to have Thomas's arms around her; but she couldn't be the one to stand in the way of his desire to leave this place and travel the world. And so she needed to harden her heart already against the wound that was to come.

'Goodbye. Look after yourself and the baby.' Sara gave Patti a hug. 'And the best of luck. With whatever the next stage brings,' she added, turning to Thorne.

He grinned. 'Yeah, well, I've just been talking to Richie Black. He was so taken with the acoustic set last night he wants us to get straight back into the studio as soon as the tour's finished. Big plans. He's going to record us as The Thornes Unplugged. We're going to have our work cut out for us come January.'

'That's fantastic news! But I hope you're going to schedule in a bit of paternity leave in February.'

'Of course, a New Man like me.'

Patti rolled her eyes. 'Yeah, well, I'll believe that when I see it. But I suppose it goes with the territory. Never get involved with a rock star, Sara.'

'I hope you're off somewhere exotic for the honeymoon?'

Patti grinned. 'Don't tell a soul. Everyone thinks we're going to Mustique, but we're really sneaking home to Sussex for a few days of peace and quiet on our own. I shall put my feet up and Thorne will be keeping me supplied with tea and Rennies . . . bliss!'

He helped her carefully into the blacked-out Mercedes that would take them to the airport and home.

Chapter 7

SOMETHING BLUE

They were still on a high after the weekend's excitement as they set to work on the changeover the following week. A little of the stardust that the Thornes and their entourage had sprinkled over the château still seemed to float on the air, the glamour and glitz vivid memories for all of them. Karen hummed a slow version of 'Perfection' as she polished the mirror in the honeymoon suite and the Héls Belles, busily making up beds, giggled as they gossiped about the celebs who'd been sleeping there.

The ring of the telephone echoed shrilly down the corridor and Sara smiled to herself as she went to answer it. All was well in the world, and peace reigned over Château Bellevue once again. Just three more weddings to go. And they should all be pretty straight-forward from here on in . . .

'Sara Cox speaking. Oh, hello, Mr Cranleigh, we're just getting everything ready for you . . .' She tailed off as the male voice at the other end of the phone stopped her mid-sentence, her light-hearted mood evaporating as she listened.

'I'm *so* sorry to hear that. Poor girl. No, please don't apologise, it's no problem at all as far as we're concerned; please don't give it another thought . . . Yes, yes of course. I totally understand. I'll see what I can do as regards the billing . . . I'll send you an email. So sorry. Yes, I know, better that she found out now than afterwards. Yes . . . okay. Goodbye.'

'That sounded heavy.' Karen set her bucket of cleaning things on the counter. 'What's up?'

Sara shook her head. 'This weekend's wedding's off.' She felt as though her heart had plummeted into the pit of her stomach, dull dread filling her at the thought of what this would do to the cash flow. 'The bride just found out that the groom's been cheating on her. They're cancelling the whole thing.'

She was trying not to panic at the thought of what this would mean for her income for the year. She needed every penny and this was a disaster.

'Oh well, at least it means you can all have a few days off.' She tried to make light of it, but the call had shaken her and her mind was a jangle of disjointed thoughts. She felt a rush of sympathy for the bride, identifying with the humiliation and heartbreak the poor girl must be feeling. And how awful, this close to the wedding – so many guests to be told, all of whom would have made travel plans . . . All that money . . . The father of the bride had sounded remarkably calm, under the circumstances.

'Oh, God. Sorry, Sara. But better she should find out now rather than later. These things do happen. Reminds me of a friend of mine in Australia who discovered her fiancé trying on her dress and shoes the day before the wedding. Stockings, garter, under-wear – the whole lot! That was another near miss, I can tell you.' Karen's grin faded. 'But what a pain for you. What happens about payment? Will you lose out?'

'Well, I need to ring round straight away and see if we're in time to cancel anything at this end for them. The caterers and the florist might not have put in their orders for the weekend yet. I can ask them, at least. Henri Dupont will keep his fee, but that's only fair as he's unlikely to get another job at such short notice.' She was thinking out loud as she pulled invoices out of the folder marked '*Cranleigh-Gordon*'.

'The wine's already bought, but we can roll that over to the next event . . . I'll work out how much I can refund the Cranleighs after I've paid the salaries. It probably won't be much, but they're not expecting anything – "a total write-off" was the phrase Mr Cranleigh used – so anything will be a bonus for the poor man.'

'Don't they have insurance? I thought you always advise people to take it out when they book?'

'Yes, but there's an exclusion clause specifically covering last-minute cancellations due to the groom being a lying, cheating bastard,' Sara said, an unintentional note of bitterness creeping into her voice.

Karen raised her eyebrows.

'Well, okay, perhaps it's not phrased in exactly those words,' Sara admitted, swallowing her anger. 'But no, under these circumstances the insurance won't cover it.'

'But your profit . . . ?'

Sara shook her head and picked up the phone. 'I'd better get on with this. Could you go and tell the girls and Antoine? If we just work up until lunchtime today then you can have the rest of the week off. You've all earned a break after last weekend in any case.'

◆ ◆ ◆

Thomas was ecstatic. She broke the news to him when he came in at lunchtime, having spent the morning checking progress in the vineyard.

'But this is wonderful news! Not for the poor bride, obviously, I'm sorry for her pain.' He brushed Sara's hair back from her face.

'But you need a break from doing things for other people, and it means I can have you to myself for once. My lovely Sara, always working so hard. You look a little tired. This is definitely good timing.' He kissed her tenderly. 'There, that's better. A smile, at last. I want to introduce you to my family. Robert and Christine will be home this week to get ready for *la rentrée* – the children go back to school soon. And my father will be home next weekend too, to start preparing everything for the harvest. They all want to meet you. And I want to show you round the vineyard. You haven't been back since that very first time when you and Gavin came to taste our wines,' he continued. 'I remember it well, this beautiful but unattainable *princesse* from Château Bellevue. I admit, I dreamed about you afterwards. And I was so happy when you rang to place your first order, as it meant I'd see you again, even if you were strictly off limits . . . There, now I've confessed: I've worshipped you from afar from the very first time I set eyes on you!'

Sara laughed. 'And now you know the reality, that the "*princesse*" spends her days scrubbing toilets and making beds in her dream château. Not to mention cooking and gardening.' She spread her work-worn hands out for his inspection and he took them in his, planting a kiss on each of her calloused palms.

'And she is all the more beautiful for it,' he said chivalrously. 'What does she have on the agenda for this afternoon?'

'Not much now. I'll have to send an email to Mr Cranleigh, but otherwise I'm completely free for once.'

'In that case, after lunch I propose to introduce you to another of our charmingly civilised French traditions, *la sieste*. Or in fact,' he went on, his lips brushing the delicate skin on the inside of her wrist, 'maybe we should make love first, then have lunch, then have our siesta again afterwards . . .' And he led her by the hand, back to the cottage, to do just that.

Sated with love and sleep, Sara reached out a lazy arm to pick up her phone. 'Don't answer it,' Thomas mumbled into her hair as he resurfaced from the depths of their afternoon siesta.

She checked the name on the screen. 'It's Dad, I'd better take it.'

'Sara, hello, we haven't spoken for a while, so I just thought I'd call and see how things are going there. Still as busy as ever?'

It was unusual for her father to ring; usually Sara called him about once a fortnight, touching base briefly and keeping up with the latest news of Lissy and Hannah. She felt pleased that he was making the effort to phone her for once, and chatted about last weekend's celebrity wedding and now the cancellation, trying not to let her anxiety about the dent to her cash flow come through in her voice. 'So it's a pain it's been cancelled, but I must admit it'll be quite nice to have a weekend off in the summer for once . . . Dad? Are you there?' She could hear her stepmother's voice in the background.

'Yes, yes, I'm here. Lissy was just saying it's a shame we're not doing anything for the long weekend. The weather's been dire here; we've hardly had any summer to speak of. So – and I'm just thinking aloud here, because of course it'll depend on what Hannah has planned . . .'

(*Of course, it always does*, thought Sara uncharitably. *Although at her age you'd have thought she'd have left home and had her own life by now . . .*)

'. . . but why don't we see if we can get a flight and come and stay? Make a few days of it. Seems a shame to waste the opportunity when you've got a château full of bedrooms standing empty!'

Suddenly Sara was wide awake, sitting up in the bed, pulling on her shirt. This was not what she'd had in mind at all. The prospect of a few precious days of holiday, preferably spent with Thomas, was receding rapidly over the horizon. She groped for an excuse, but failed to come up with any credible reason why they shouldn't come and stay.

'That sounds lovely, Dad,' she said, her forced enthusiasm sounding hollow to her ears.

'Great. It'll be good to see you – we've been worried about how you're coping with Gavin out of the picture.' She smiled wanly at this. 'We'll check with Hannah and go and look at flights straight away. I'll call you back . . .'

Sara groaned as she flopped back on to the pillow beside Thomas. He opened one eye and grinned at her. 'Yay! Family!' he joked, poking her in the ribs.

She closed her eyes. 'Ugh. Just when I was looking forward to staying in bed for a week with my hot French lover . . . Oh well, maybe all the flights will be fully booked.' She opened her eyes again and turned to face him. 'You must think I'm a really horrible daughter, not wanting them to come.'

He traced a finger lightly down her nose and then tapped gently on the tip. 'No. Not at all. I know you're not a horrible person, so there must be a good reason why you don't want them here. Don't worry, I know you have a complicated family. I've got step-brothers and sisters myself, remember.'

She sighed. 'It's just . . . with them everything always seems to be about Hannah. And it's the same on Mum's side. She's always been preoccupied with Roger's children – he was a widower when she met him and so she stepped into the role of their mother. I suppose they really did need her though, having lost their own mum so young. I always feel guilty for envying them and begrudging them my mother's attention.' She shook her head. 'When Mum and Dad got divorced, I felt I didn't belong to either of them any more. I wasn't special to anyone. Except my grandfather.' Her expression softened as she remembered him. Thomas listened, watching her face intently. 'I used to be packed off to spend the school holidays with my grandparents and I kind of latched on to him. He was a keen gardener and I used to follow him around, helping him to dig and weed. I was probably just getting in his way really, but he was always so patient and kind. It was from him that I learned how to garden. I think of him whenever I'm out there.' She nodded towards the window, where the Madame Alfred Carrière roses that framed it cascaded, a creamy froth against their dark green foliage, and fell silent.

'And where is he now?' Thomas prompted gently, still holding her in his arms.

'He died a few years ago. Went into hospital for a minor operation and caught an infection. He never came out.' She was quiet for a moment, remembering. 'He would have loved it here. I know he'd have approved of what I've done so far. And he'd have been so excited about my plans for the gardens.' *Which are never going to happen now*, she stopped herself from adding.

The phone chirped again beside her. 'Hi, Dad.'

'Well, we've booked ourselves on the Bordeaux flight on Friday. So lucky, we got the last four seats – oh, yes, I hope that's okay, Hannah's bringing a friend. They were going to spend the day at the sea, but this'll be even more fun for them. The tickets were pretty pricey at this late stage but, as Lissy said, it's not as if it's costing us anything at the other end . . . Can you come and meet us? Our flight gets in at midday. Great – can't wait to see you. How lucky that you had that cancellation!'

Sara rang off and turned back to Thomas. 'Yay! Family!' she echoed faintly.

He propped himself up on one elbow and kissed her forehead where it had contracted into a slight frown. 'Don't worry. It'll be fine. You'll introduce me to your family and I'll introduce you to mine. A big week! I've got a good idea,' he continued. 'There's a *marché nocturne* at Saussignac on Saturday night – let's all go. It's great fun – all the local *producteurs* have stalls with different foods and wines. And there's dancing. Not that the DJ will be up to the very high standards of Château Bellevue, of course. I doubt he's ever done a party for a world-famous rock band!'

'Why, Thomas Cortini! I do believe your fame is quite going to your head,' Sara laughed.

'Not at all, I am very modest. Now, prepare to be made love to once again by the world's greatest disc jockey and winemaker!'

'How lovely! I can't wait to meet them both . . .' But Sara's teasing was smothered as Thomas's lips met hers.

As she leaned against the kitchen counter, waiting for the croissants to warm in the oven, Sara massaged the knots in her neck and shoulders. She'd tried to stay relaxed about having her dad and his family here, but within the first few minutes of their arrival she'd felt the customary tightening in her jaw as she gritted her teeth in a fixed smile, listening politely to her stepmother's stream of chatter. 'We were so disappointed to hear your engagement was off! Hannah was looking forward to being a bridesmaid, weren't you, Hannah?'

From the back seat of the car, where she and her friend were both engrossed in their phones, catching up on some hot-and-heavy texting, having been disconnected from the world for all of an hour on the flight over, Hannah had grunted.

'Anyway, never mind. Her cousin Amanda's getting married next spring, so that's made up for it. Ooh, are those grapes? I never knew they grew like that. And we're really looking forward to seeing your château. Hannah looked it up on the internet, didn't you, Hannah, before we booked the flights. It looks very smart . . .'

Sara felt her shoulders steadily ratchet themselves up towards her ears as Lissy rattled on, all the way back to Coulliac.

'. . . And Hannah and Amy, you're in here,' Sara had said, throwing open the door to one of the prettiest bedrooms, a twin-bedded room with a view of the barn and the pool.

'Oh, are we supposed to share? I haven't slept in a single bed for years,' Hannah had complained.

'Well, yes, I thought you'd probably prefer to be together.' And it would also be one less room to clean next week; having already done the changeover, she was hoping to minimise the amount of work they'd need to do to prepare for the next wedding.

And then this morning, instead of a leisurely Saturday morning lie-in for once during the season, she'd got up early and gone down to the bakery to buy croissants and fresh bread for their breakfast, quietly closing the cottage door behind her as she slipped out, leaving Thomas asleep in bed. 'This is weird,' he'd commented the night before. 'You sleep in the cottage while they are installed in your best bedrooms in the château. I thought Cinderella was a character in a fairy story, but it seems she's still alive today and living in Château Bellevue.'

'Oh well, it's simpler this way. I can't be bothered moving back just for the weekend when all my things are here. I shall reclaim my castle soon enough at the end of the season.' *Though heaven knows how long it'll be mine*, she thought. She was still waiting for the bank manager to get back from holiday, desperately hoping he'd agree to loan her the money she needed to buy out Gavin's share. It was her last chance to keep the château.

Sara dragged her attention back to Thomas as she lay in bed beside him. 'And anyway, I may be Cinderella, but luckily my prince doesn't mind slumming it in the cottage with me!'

Thomas had turned to her. 'So am I your prince, Sara?' He was serious suddenly, so she deflected his question lightly.

'Of course. Until I send you out into the big wide world to slay a few dragons. I wouldn't want you to think I was a complete pushover.'

Tonight he was taking them all to the night market at Saussignac, so that should keep her family happy and it meant she didn't need to shop for supper and cook.

'Good morning, Dad, Lissy. I hope you slept well?'

'Yes, fine, thanks. It's very quiet here, isn't it? Hannah came through in the night though, because Amy was snoring and it was keeping her awake. So I told her just to move to one of the other bedrooms. They all seemed to be made up so it wasn't a problem. And she does prefer a double bed.'

I will not be made to feel guilty. I will not get annoyed at my step-mother. I will not be jealous of my stepsister . . . Sara's shoulders had now welded themselves to her ears with tension and she couldn't help crashing the coffee pot down on to the table with more force than was strictly necessary.

But then Thomas came into the kitchen and wrapped his arms around her. 'Aah!' He sniffed the air appreciatively. 'The servants have already made our breakfast – how wonderful!'

'Oh, do you have help even at the weekends?' Lissy bit into a warm croissant, thickly spread with butter and jam. 'Well, it's all right for some, isn't it!'

Sara bared her teeth at Thomas in a mock snarl that no one else could see, but his amused smile and the understanding sparkle in his eyes did make her shoulders relax downwards an inch or two, and she suddenly felt a lot better, having someone beside her who understood what she was really feeling.

The night air was warm as they strolled into the pretty village of Saussignac. People had come from far and wide, and they'd had to park the cars some way from the central square alongside the elegant château that dominated the main street.

The sound of laughter and the heady scents of garlic and chip-fat were drawing a steady stream of revellers towards long trestle tables set out beneath a canopy of lime trees. Thomas held Sara's hand as they walked beside her father and stepmother and Antoine and Héloise, who had cadged a lift in Thomas's van since they'd needed to take two cars and there were places to spare. Hannah and Amy, still engrossed with their phones, brought up the rear.

Saussignac's tree-lined square nestled beneath the elegant spire of the village church, and, under the canopy of leaves, stalls had been set up on two sides of the *place*. Cheerful queues were forming as people lined up for oysters or *moules-frites*, steaks or *magret de canard*. Several local winemakers were displaying their wares and doing a roaring trade.

Sara's attention was caught by a group seated at one of the long tables who were waving animatedly, several bottles of wine open before them. She nudged Thomas, who was busy explaining the offerings at each of the stalls to Lissy and the girls (accompanied by protestations of 'Oysters? Yuck!' 'Eew, mussels!' 'I never eat duck . . .').

'Aha! They're here already. Come and meet my family. And Gina and Cédric too.'

The introductions and customary two-kisses-per-person took some time to complete. 'My brother, Robert, and his wife, Christine. My father, Patrick. And Cédric and Gina Thibault, the uncle and aunt of Hélène and Héloise.'

Gina hugged Sara warmly. 'I've been looking forward to meeting you. Thomas has told us so much about you!'

'He has indeed.' Patrick Cortini, dashing with his white hair and neatly groomed moustache, embraced Sara with enthusiasm. 'Another beautiful *Anglaise* who is stealing the hearts of our local men . . . It is truly the English taking their revenge for the Norman Conquest!'

'Yes, and you need to release Sara now, Papa,' said Thomas, reclaiming her for himself. 'You already have your own English girlfriend, remember?'

'And you don't want me reporting back to my mother that you've been two-timing her!' joked Gina.

'It was Gina's mother that Papa was visiting,' Thomas explained. 'She's coming over soon in return, to help with the harvest.'

Gina smiled. 'I hope you're not expecting her to shovel grape skins and scrub out vats though. I think what she has in mind is more along the lines of helping Christine with the cooking and playing with her grandchildren.'

'How many children do you have?' Sara asked.

'Three. Luc and Nathalie are my stepchildren and we have baby Pierre. He's one and a half, toddling around and getting into everything. It's a good job he's got his besotted grandmother and his adoring half-brother and sister to lend a hand with looking after him or I'd be a complete basket case. They're babysitting tonight, to give us a night off, which is utter bliss!'

Another complex family, Sara mused. She warmed to Gina instantly.

'Come and sit down. We were just tasting a range of the wines on offer tonight. We're in the Bergerac *appellation* here and there are some very interesting local organic producers.'

'Ah, Gina, do you never stop working?' teased Thomas fondly.

'You know me, Thomas, totally selfless in the eternal quest for delicious wines. It's a tough job!'

They settled themselves down, joining the noisy throng, and Thomas poured glasses of wine for each of them. The noise level increased steadily in directly inverse relation to the falling level of wine in the bottles. Darkness fell and the strings of fairy lights in the branches above them began to twinkle. Sara glanced down the table, to where her father and Lissy were deep in conversation with Patrick and Robert, who were eager to share their passion for winemaking and to describe the coming harvest. At the other end, Antoine and Héloise were laughing as they exchanged new phrases in English and French with Hannah and Amy, who – Sara was impressed to note – had even put their phones away, the better to enjoy their supper.

She couldn't remember ever having felt so relaxed at a family meal. Back in England, she associated such gatherings with a sense of tension as she negotiated the undercurrents of hurt, resentment and jealousy that still lurked like jagged rocks just below the surface on both sides of her fractured family, usually resulting in a severe case of indigestion by the time the meal drew to a close. But here, the assembled company ebbed and flowed good-naturedly as people got up to visit the stalls for another delicious course of whatever looked tempting. There was much sharing of dishes. And Hannah was even heard to say, 'Oh my God! Duck is *so* my new favourite thing! Who knew it was so delicious? We definitely need to have this at home, Mum.' Which was about the longest and most effusive speech Sara had ever heard her make.

The others were teasing Thomas about his newfound DJ-ing skills, and he was filling them in with snippets of gossip from his recent brush with rock royalty.

Gina turned to Sara. 'I hear you've done an amazing job at Château Bellevue. Thomas has told us how lovely it's looking, especially the gardens.'

'Thanks. You'll have to come and see it. It's not finished though – I've still got big plans for the landscaping, if I'm still here next year. I hope I can see it through. I have this sense of needing to do it justice. I'm not sure why. Just that its history somehow deserves it, even though I don't know much about it.'

Gina nodded. 'It *does* have quite a history, or so I've heard. My mother-in-law, Mireille, might be able to tell you more. Her family used to own the old mill on the river below the château – where Christine's parents now live.' She nodded up the table towards Robert's wife. 'Mireille grew up there – it must have been around the 1930s, because I know she went to work in Paris in her late teens and was there in the war years. But her parents and her younger sister were living in the *moulin* up until the end of the Second World War, so I'm sure she'd have some stories to tell. Not that people round here like talking about the war much. I suppose it's a period they'd rather forget on the whole.'

'I'd love to meet her sometime. And if she could tell me anything more about the château then that'd be great.'

Gina leaned in towards Sara so that she could hear her above the cacophony of chatter and laughter that swirled louder around them as music began to blare from the speakers flanking the church.

'It can't have been easy, having to keep going after your fiancé left. You must be exhausted by this stage in the season.'

'A bit,' Sara admitted. 'But, you know, at the same time I'm finding that I've still really enjoyed trying to make a go of it. And of course, Thomas has been a lifesaver – in more ways than one!'

Gina laughed, but then her expression grew serious again as she asked, 'So *do* you think you'll still be here next year?'

Sara shrugged. 'It's a bit complicated. I really don't know at the moment, but I don't want to think about it for a few more weeks until the season's over. It depends on several things.'

'Is one of the "things" Thomas?' Gina's voice was low, and she looked directly into Sara's eyes as she asked this, watching her intently.

Sara dropped her gaze. How could she admit to someone she'd only just met this evening something that she wasn't even prepared to admit to herself? She glanced down the table again at her dad and her stepmother; her father was handing over some more cash to Hannah and Amy so that they could go and get *crêpes au chocolat* for dessert.

She knew from experience that when you want something in life, it usually leads to bitter disappointment when you can't have it. So she'd long ago tried to stop herself from wanting anything too much. The château, her business, the plans for the garden. Thomas. She knew they could soon all go the same way as her other longings: her longing for a home, or at least a place where she would be welcome when there was nowhere else for her to go; her longing for a family that no longer existed; her longing for a dream wedding of her own that had evaporated in the cold light of day with Gavin's departure.

Raising her eyes to meet Gina's candid gaze now, she deflected the heaviness of the question with a smile. 'Ah, well, we'll have to see. Thomas will most probably be on tour as the warm-up act for The Steel Thornes by then.'

The two women grinned, as they turned to where Cédric and Robert were now teasing Thomas about his taste in music, guffawing with laughter and clapping him on the back.

Thomas noticed they were looking at him. 'Uh-oh.' He nudged Cédric. 'A couple of hot English girls are giving us the eye. Do you think we should ask them to dance?'

'For sure.' Cédric grinned back at them. 'I'll take the blonde, you take the brunette . . .'

◆ ◆ ◆

Having been whirled around the dance floor by Thomas, and waltzed around somewhat more decorously by his father, Sara felt she'd well and truly worked off her supper by the time they wandered back to the cars at the end of the evening. Progress was slow, with frequent stops to say goodnight to people who knew Thomas and his family, most of whom seemed especially interested to check Sara out. She realised that word of their relationship had most definitely got around already in the local community.

As Gina said goodnight, she hugged Sara once more. 'It's been great meeting you at long last. Let's get together again soon.'

Sara smiled to herself as she got into the car; she felt she'd met a kindred spirit and she was definitely looking forward to getting to know Gina better.

Thomas tooted the horn as he pulled away. Hannah and Amy, giggling happily, had opted to join Antoine and Héloise on the bench seats in the back of the van on the way home.

'What a lovely evening,' her father said, climbing into the passenger seat beside her. 'I do like your new friends. And what a character old Patrick Cortini is!'

And Sara felt a sudden lightness of heart and a surge of affection for her family; dysfunctional it may have been, but perhaps it was no more dysfunctional than anyone else's these days. The mixture of three generations and two cultures in the simple setting of the village market had turned out to be the recipe for a perfect evening. *Thanks to you, Thomas*, she thought.

◆ ◆ ◆

She hurried back from seeing her family off at the airport in order to tidy and clean up after them, so that there'd be a minimum of

113

work for the team to do in preparation for the next weekend's wedding. Thomas had left to go over to Château de la Chapelle, helping Robert and his father make a start with the preparations for the harvest. She hummed as she remade the beds, shaking out the crisply laundered sheets that smelled of fresh air and sunshine and smoothing down the pretty bedcovers.

Suddenly she paused, listening. For a moment she thought she'd heard voices outside. She opened the window and leaned out. And then, jumping with shock, she nearly lost her balance and fell headlong out of the window and on to the ground below as she realised that Gavin was standing there beneath her, accompanied by the estate agent who'd helped them buy the château two years before.

Shaking with rage, she hurried downstairs, trying to gather her thoughts. 'Monsieur Bonneval.' She held out a hand to the agent. 'And Gavin too.' She didn't bother holding out her hand to him. 'Well, this *is* a surprise.'

'Hello, Sara.' He took half a step towards her, as if he was about to kiss her cheek, but Sara folded her arms and leaned away almost imperceptibly, the agent's presence preventing her from telling Gavin what she really felt like saying. Anger coursed through her veins like molten lava.

Oblivious, the estate agent looked about him. 'What a transformation! I'm looking forward to seeing inside too, now you've finished the work,' he enthused. 'I'm delighted to take this property on again and in fact I just may have a client who'd be interested. Depending on your asking price, of course. I'm afraid it's still very much a buyer's market at the moment.'

'I know, but that can't be helped,' said Gavin, his usual assured self, smoothly taking charge. 'I need the money out. Bit of a change of plans' – he avoided looking Sara in the eye – 'so I'd be open to offers, within reason, of course.'

His use of the word 'I' made Sara's hackles rise.

'Well, this client is going to be here next week. He's looking for a possible business opportunity in France that he and his wife could run. I'll put together some particulars and send them through to him, but I imagine he'll be keen to see Château Bellevue while he's here. It's just the sort of property they're thinking of.'

Sara felt her throat constricting, her heart pounding at the thought of losing the château. That old feeling, that she was losing her voice when in Gavin's company, came flooding back. He'd walked back in here so brazenly, after everything he'd done, and taken over again.

She tried to speak, but only a hoarse croak emerged. The agent began to snap a few photos as Gavin pointed out the landscaping that they'd done. That *she'd* done. Her garden. Her home.

She cleared her throat. 'No,' she said.

The two men carried on, as if she hadn't spoken. She marched over to Monsieur Bonneval and caught hold of his arm as he raised the camera to take a picture of the pergola-framed view. 'No.' She cleared her throat again, her voice stronger now. 'It's not for sale.'

The smile on the estate agent's face froze and his eyes flickered with confusion. 'But Gavin . . . ?' he asked, swivelling his head from one to the other.

'I'm buying Gavin out. Château Bellevue is not for sale, Monsieur Bonneval. I'm very sorry you have had a wasted journey. It would have been better if Monsieur Farrell had called first, since he no longer lives here. As he so rightly says, there's been a change of plan.'

Just then, Thomas's van pulled up. He blinked as he took in the scene before him, doing a double take at the sight of Gavin, sensing Sara's angry tension. He climbed out and came over to stand alongside her, and she was grateful for his gesture of solidarity. His presence at her side gave her a sense of strength. She wasn't going to give up the château without a fight, so it was good to feel she had someone backing her up as she fought her corner. She'd never felt so sure of anything before in her life.

'Thomas?' Gavin said, disconcerted.

Thomas nodded coolly. 'Gavin.'

The estate agent looked from Gavin to Sara and back again, then shrugged. 'Ah well, I'll leave you to sort it out between you. If I can be of help at any stage, Mademoiselle Cox, please don't hesitate to call.'

Gavin glowered, angry that Monsieur Bonneval had deferred to her. 'I want my money, Sara.' His voice was low, but held an unmistakeable threat.

'I'll get it,' she said, her own voice firm and clear. 'Give me until the end of the season. That's the very least you can do. I'm not selling.'

Sara and Thomas stood together in silence and watched as the two men drove off down the hill. Then Thomas put an arm around her and she leaned her forehead against the broad firmness of his chest, her legs shaking suddenly. She had a hollow feeling in the pit of her stomach at the thought of what she'd done. She still hadn't been able to contact the bank manager to find out whether a loan might even be a possibility. He should be back in the office tomorrow, so she'd ring him first thing to try and set up an appointment. But what if . . . ?

Thomas kissed her hair, and she looked up anxiously into his face.

He took her by the hand. 'Come. Don't look so worried. Let's go and look at the view and you can tell me what's going on.'

They sat, hand in hand, gazing out across the valley, and she told him about the letter from Gavin demanding his money back and her determination not to be bullied into selling. She now knew she had so very much to lose.

When she was all talked out, she turned and smiled sorrowfully at him. 'Thanks for listening, Thomas. I know there's nothing you can do to help sort out my problems, but it feels better having shared them with you.'

He took her in his arms again. 'Oh, my poor Sara. You carry so much on these slender shoulders of yours, don't you?' He thought for a moment. 'And actually, there *is* something I can do. I think I can at least help you get an appointment with the bank manager. Charles Dupuy was in the same year at school as my brother, Robert, so I know him well. And I'll come to the meeting with you too, if you like.' He held up his hands as she began to protest. 'I know, I know! You are fiercely independent and perfectly capable of going alone, and your French is good enough to understand what's being said. But perhaps at a time like this it would be nice to have a friend at your side? For moral support, if nothing else.'

Sara smiled and nodded slowly, reluctantly admitting to herself that it would, in fact, probably be helpful to have him there. She doubted she'd know all the right financial vocabulary, and Thomas would be a good ally to have when it came to tackling the inevitable daunting French bureaucracy that would undoubtedly ensue if she could actually persuade the bank manager to give her the loan.

'Anyway,' Thomas said reassuringly, 'surely you're making such a success of your business that they'll lend you the money?'

She nodded slowly, doubts creeping in. 'I'll have to show them the detailed figures. This season looks okay, I think, given that it was our first, although last week's cancellation certainly doesn't help the bottom line. But I don't have a single firm booking for next year yet, so that will count against me. If I have to sell, though, I'll lose out big time. The agent said that property prices have fallen since we bought the château.'

'And would you really *want* to sell?' Thomas's voice was level, his tone carefully light.

Sara looked back at the château, her fortress, solid on its hilltop, and she felt, once again, a visceral sense of belonging here. It felt so right to be in this place. With this man. Feelings that she'd never in her life experienced with such certainty. Her eyes filled with tears, and her unspoken emotion threatened to overwhelm her. She blinked to clear her vision but, before she could stop it, a single tear spilled on to her cheek.

Thomas wiped it away with his fingertips. 'I see,' he said, with a tender smile. And it seemed to Sara that a new light of hope flickered in his eyes for a moment. 'So we need to persuade the bank manager what an excellent proposition Château Bellevue de Coulliac is and secure that loan. For all our sakes. *Allons-y.* Let's go and have a glass of wine while we prepare our business case for tomorrow.'

She regained her composure and kissed him on the lips. 'Thomas Cortini. Thank you for being here.'

◆ ◆ ◆

Monsieur Dupuy listened carefully as Sara presented her business plan, jotting down occasional notes on the pad on the desk in front of him. As promised, Thomas had phoned him first thing in the morning and managed to set up a meeting for that very afternoon.

When she'd finished talking, the bank manager leaned back in his chair, stretching out his arms and interlocking his fingers in an unconscious gesture that gave Sara the distinct impression he was physically fending off her hopes and dreams. His smile was warm, his expression kind – but his body language told a different story.

'I appreciate your plan, Mademoiselle Cox, and all the hard work you are doing at Château Bellevue de Coulliac to make a go of your business. Your weddings certainly bring economic benefits to the local area. If it was up to me, I'd happily give you the loan you are seeking. But a case such as this I will need to present to our head office in Paris. And I don't wish to disappoint you but, as I think you know, banks are not in a very generous mood at the moment when it comes to lending money. The fact that you are seeking to underwrite such a large proportion of your business' – he reached for his pad to check his notes – 'sixty per cent, was it? – does not help. If it were a lesser amount, or if you had a track record of a few more years, then the case might be stronger. But with only one year's figures, and nothing definite in the diary for next season, and because we live in very uncertain times, I suspect the powers that be will view this proposition with caution.'

He shrugged, turning to Thomas. 'I promise you I will do my best, but I don't want Mademoiselle Cox to be too disappointed if the loan is not approved.' He stood, shaking their hands and ushering them to the door. 'Either way, I'll let you know by the end of the week.'

Sara and Thomas were silent in the car on the way home, each lost in their own thoughts. As they pulled into the drive, Sara looked up at her château and felt something switch off inside, her sense of ownership already diminishing as she saw her dreams slipping through her fingers. The in-built safety valve that she'd cultivated through life's disappointments was already making her begin to distance herself in self-defence.

She parked the car by the cottage and turned off the engine, and the two of them sat in silence for a moment longer. Then, as if reading her mind, Thomas reached out and took both her hands in his. '*Courage*, Sara. Don't give up yet. There is still a chance the loan will come through.'

She nodded, wanting to believe this was true, but thinking that she already knew, in her heart of hearts, what the bank's answer would be.

◆ ◆ ◆

That night, Thomas drove her over to Château de la Chapelle for supper. 'Papa wants to know why I'm hiding you away from the family and insists we come and sit at his table tonight. Robert and Christine will be there too. And, indeed, Christine will be cooking, which is good news as my father's culinary efforts usually involve setting fire to something he has shot. And as the hunting season doesn't start again for a few more weeks, all he has left in the freezer at this time of year is a rabbit or two and possibly a pigeon.'

Sara was pleased to be included and was looking forward to seeing Robert and Christine again; there hadn't been much opportunity to talk to them at the Saussignac market, but she had come away with an impression of their easy warmth and ready sense of humour, as well as their kindness in including her own family in the conversation at that end of the table.

She'd been to the Cortinis' vineyard before several times to buy wine, but this was the first time she'd had a chance to go there with Thomas. He pointed out the smaller house to one side of the main building, where Robert and Christine lived with their three children. 'For the moment, Papa still rules the roost, living in the main house, and, as the unmarried son, I'm still in the bedroom I had as a child. When I'm not in *your* bedroom, that is.'

'You've lived in this house all your life?' asked Sara. 'That's amazing.'

He shrugged. 'It's not so unusual around here. Especially where you have family estates. Why, how many different places have you lived in?'

Sara tallied them up in her head. 'Five and a half – no, six and a half before I came here.'

He grinned. 'A half? You've lived in half a place?'

'No, I've half-lived in a place. When my father married Lissy, I went there every other weekend and some holidays. But it certainly never felt like home. By that time, neither did my mother's place, as she'd married my stepfather. He was a widower and she moved in with him and his children. It felt like they took her over, as she made such an effort to fill in for the mother they'd lost. She just never really had much time left over for me. And they are quite a bit younger than me, so I was expected to help look after them too. It felt like, at that point, I could no longer be a child myself. Whatever I might have felt about the divorce and all the changes that were going on around me got buried.'

'How old were you when all this took place?' Thomas's gaze was compassionate.

'Ten. I used to try to find reasons to stay late at school – I volunteered for drama, sport, library duty, anything that kept me out of the house.'

Thomas shook his head. 'That's tough. We were lucky, I suppose, that my mother only left when we were in our late teens, so we were more independent. We never once doubted that this was our home.' He smiled at her. 'Maybe you think I'm being very ungrateful to want to leave all this – when you want your home so much and it's under threat?'

Sara reflected for a moment. 'I think perhaps it's *because* you have such a secure home that you feel you can go. It's like diving – you need a firm base from which to launch yourself, otherwise you can't take off. I'd floated here and there with no strong sense of direction until I came to Château Bellevue. But now I do feel I have a solid base there. I don't want to give it up yet. The feeling of being rooted, for the first time in my life, is such a powerful one: I think it's given me a much stronger sense of myself, more confidence in my capabilities. Still, at least now I have my springboard, if I can just find the courage to relaunch myself when the time comes.'

Thomas took her hand. 'Perhaps we will dive together, as we did that day at the weir.'

For a moment, Sara contemplated the thought of travelling with him, footloose, through the world, no fixed abode. In her heart of hearts, she knew that wasn't what she wanted. A childhood of being rootless meant that, now she could decide for herself, she would choose to find a home again in a heartbeat.

Before she could find the words to reply, Patrick Cortini emerged from the château, arms spread wide in welcome, and they climbed out of the van to greet him.

'Lovely Sara' – he kissed her hand gallantly – 'welcome to my humble home! As you can see, it's nothing like as grand as your own château, but we make do here.'

'It's such a beautiful spot.' She looked about her. 'It feels as if the hillside is holding the farm in its arms. The church spire is so pretty on the skyline there. And your vineyard looks immaculate.'

'Well, we have Robert to thank for that. The vines are his passion. He only allows Thomas and me to drive a tractor very occasionally.'

'Yes, or to help with the really tough jobs, like the pruning,' Thomas chipped in. 'Although even then he keeps coming to check I'm doing it right. He's a real chip off the old block.' He nudged his father fondly.

Patrick's passionate and somewhat technical explanation of pruning techniques, which then ensued, was interrupted by the appearance of Robert and Christine in the doorway.

'*Bonsoir*, Sara,' Christine smiled. 'Come, let's go and have a glass of wine before these three try to take you on a tour of the entire vineyard before dinner.'

In the garden on the far side of the house, she introduced Sara to her sons, who were throwing a ball to each other, hindered by the enthusiastic interventions of a friendly collie whose tail never stopped wagging as it ran between them, its tongue lolling happily.

They settled down at a table under the generous canopy of an ancient walnut tree, a cloud of birds – and even a red squirrel – that had been raiding the green-cased kernels departing in haste as they approached. Thomas pulled the cork from a perfectly chilled bottle and poured glasses of the château's crisp white wine for each of them, while Christine passed round slices of dried sausage and a bowl of plump olives.

'*À table!*' she called to the boys. The three of them came running and pulled up chairs. 'But come and wash your hands first! And you can help me carry.'

Sara got up to lend a hand, but Christine patted her arm and shooed her back to the table, saying, 'You spend your days doing things for others. Have a night off.'

'Now, Sara, come and sit here by me,' Patrick gestured. 'I want to hear all about the work you've done at Château Bellevue. Thomas tells us your passion is the garden?'

The old man seemed genuinely interested, his bright eyes watching her shrewdly from beneath his bushy white eyebrows as she described the renovations and the way she ran the business. Robert and Christine listened too, asking questions of their own occasionally, and Thomas chipped in every now and then when he thought Sara was being too modest about her achievements, or had left anything out.

Sara found herself opening up, more than she'd intended to, about the financial impasse she now faced, her tongue loosened, no doubt, by the encouraging combination of wine, food and company as she tucked into the plate of *carbonnade* Christine had put in front of her, a delicious pork stew laced with thyme and the earthy richness of wild mushrooms.

Old Patrick chuckled as she ran through the different weddings they'd hosted at Château Bellevue that season. 'Who'd ever have thought our little corner of the world would attract such a variety of people! The old château has witnessed much history in its time, through times of peace and darker times of war and sadness. How wonderful that now it's the setting for so much happiness. I like the idea of your business, Mam'selle Sara, bringing people's dreams to life. Let's hope that young pen-pusher at the bank succeeds in persuading his smart Parisian colleagues to invest. Times are hard, but if anyone deserves a chance, it's you. You bring the world to our door, buy our wines, provide employment. And, best of all, you've kept my son happy and busy this summer.' He rumpled Thomas's hair. '*Une femme merveilleuse!*'

They drove home in silence, Sara contentedly sleepy and replete. She realised that something was different tonight. Instead of her habitual sense of being on the outside looking in, her nose pressed against the sweetshop window, the Cortinis had thrown open the door and invited her in. For one happy evening, she'd felt included.

She drew her knees up and turned in the passenger seat to look at Thomas, his square jaw and aquiline profile lit by the glow of the van's dashboard lights. He seemed lost in thoughts of his own. Becoming aware that she was watching him, he glanced at her and his serious expression melted with his slow smile. 'What?'

She shook her head. 'Nothing.' A pause. And then, 'I love your family, that's all.'

She was silent again for a moment and then said, 'Almost as much as I love you.'

Looking straight ahead at the road again, Thomas nodded. And after another moment he said seriously, 'Coming from a girl who keeps her heart locked away in a tall tower, surrounded by a forest of thorns, that's quite an admission.'

She dropped her gaze again. Without taking his eyes off the road, he reached over and took her hand in his. 'I love you too, Sara.'

Her eyes filmed over with tears. And then, carefully, looking straight ahead now herself, she replied, 'You do know me well, Thomas Cortini.'

Chapter 8

SOMETHING OLD

Sara set down the tin of furniture polish and hurried into the hallway to answer the phone. She was delighted to hear Gina's voice at the other end of the line.

'You remember at the night market I mentioned that my mother-in-law, Mireille, might be able to tell you a bit more about the château's history? Well, her sister, Eliane, is visiting her today. I told them about our conversation, and they'd be happy to come and meet you. So I wondered whether we could seize the moment and come over this afternoon. Only if it suits you, of course. If it's not convenient at such short notice then we can always organise it for another time.'

'Today would be fine,' Sara smiled, welcoming the distraction from her anxiety about waiting for the bank manager's phone call. 'Come for tea. It'll be lovely to meet them both. And to see you again too.' Then the name of Mireille's sister registered with her. 'Hang on a minute. Is Eliane married to someone called Mathieu Dubosq?'

'She is. How did you know that?' Gina asked.

Sara explained about the names she'd found in the register of marriages.

'How perfect!' Gina exclaimed. 'I'm sure they'd love to see that. See you later then.'

They arrived promptly at three thirty, the doors of Gina's little car opening to disgorge two of her children – her stepdaughter, Nathalie, and her baby son, Pierre – as well as the two elderly ladies.

Mireille was obviously the elder sister, dressed in black, her slight frame bent with age as she leaned on a stick to help her walk, but her eyes were bright and she glanced about sharply, taking in the château and its grounds and appraising Sara in one piercing sweep. Eliane was a little taller, less stooped than Mireille. Her pure white hair was twisted into a simple knot at the nape of her neck and a few strands had escaped, blowing across her face as she stood for a few moments gazing out at the view, slightly apart from the others, who were busy with greetings and introductions. When she finally turned to take Sara's hand, the expression in her clear grey eyes seemed a little distant, as if Eliane were seeing things other than the cluster of women and children in front of her, her head cocked slightly to one side as though she were listening to voices other than those of Sara, Gina and Mireille. Could she hear the voices of ghosts, mingling with the laughter of Nathalie and little Pierre as they ran across the lawn to play on the swing set on the far side? That was the impression Sara had. She invited them to take a seat on the terrace and brought out the tea things, setting the old photo album and the leather-bound ledger alongside them.

Eliane smiled at the jug of blue and white cottage-garden flowers on the table. '*Cosméa, bourrache, bleuet . . .*' She named each one, gently touching the petals with her fingertips. She lingered over the sky-blue cornflowers. 'The *bleuet* is the French symbol for those who have given their lives in times of war, you know. You English use the poppy to remember; we use the cornflower. They grow side by side on the battlefield, the first flowers to regrow. New life. New hope, after all that destruction.'

'Eliane knows everything there is to know about gardening,' Gina explained. 'She's an expert on wildflowers and knows where to find the best wild mushrooms.'

Eliane looked at Sara, her eyes more clearly focused on her now. 'You grow these here, in the gardens at the château?' Her speech was slow and considered, making it easy for Sara to understand, even through the strong local accent that gave the words a twanging edge.

Sara nodded. '*Oui*. When I came here, the gardens were completely overgrown. I've made a start, but there's still work to do, both landscaping and planting.'

'My sister used to work here at Château Bellevue,' Mireille chimed in, 'in the kitchen mostly but sometimes in the garden too. Especially the *potager*.'

Sara reached for the album of photographs. 'I thought that might be the case.' She smiled, showing Eliane the picture of the young girl standing beside the beehives. 'Is this you, by any chance?'

A look of wonderment spread over Eliane's face. 'Why, yes, it is. Look, Mireille, it's the Comte's pictures. I thought these had been lost!'

The two women pored over the album, pointing out people and places they remembered from long ago.

'I found this too,' Sara said, showing them the page in the ledger where Eliane and Mathieu's marriage had been entered in 1945.

Eliane traced the words with her forefinger. 'The priest must have written this. It's not the Comte's handwriting, you see? He was gone by then.' Her expression clouded over, as if a mist had drawn a veil across the sun. 'In the war, this château was occupied by the Germans. Those were terrible years.'

Sara turned to Eliane. 'When exactly was it that you worked here at the château?'

There was a pause. The old lady's grey eyes seemed to focus once again on scenes from a time and a place in the distant past, as if she were watching things that were invisible to the rest of them.

'I worked in the kitchens for about three years,' she replied finally. 'From when I was sixteen until I was nineteen.'

'It was during the war,' Mireille elaborated. 'Nineteen forty-one to nineteen forty-four. I'd left home to go and do my apprenticeship in Paris, just before the Second World War broke out. Eliane worked here at Château Bellevue as an assistant to the cook. Our parents lived in the old *moulin* on the river: our father ran our small farm as well as the mill, and our mother was a *sage-femme*.' She turned to Gina for help translating this.

'A midwife. It literally means "wise-woman".'

Mireille nodded. 'Our mother knew all about using herbs and plants as medicine. It's from her that Eliane gained a lot of her knowledge.'

'So you were here when the Germans were, during the war?' Sara had the impression that Eliane's expression changed slightly, becoming even more guarded, darkness falling across her features. She didn't reply.

Sara reminded herself what Thomas had said, as well as Gina's gentle warning that night in Saussignac, that people around here didn't really like talking about the war years much. She realised she probably shouldn't be asking so many questions.

Mireille glanced at her sister, then replied for her. 'The Germans took over the château in nineteen forty-three. This area was right on the edge of occupied France at the time and they wanted to use it as a command post. They broadcast pro-German and pro-Vichy propaganda from here by radio. But Monsieur le Comte stayed on, living in the cottage. And Eliane and one or two other staff continued to work here too.'

'I found a Nazi jacket stuffed into the wall in the cottage,' Sara said eagerly. 'I think it must have dated back to those times?'

Eliane nodded. 'They departed in a hurry when the war was ending. All sorts of things were left behind. After the Comte's death, the château stood empty for many years, with just a care-taker living in the cottage. I suppose he made use of whatever was to hand when it came to keeping warm. I know he had to do some work on the cottage to make it habitable.'

Sara nodded. 'That would explain the blankets I found there too.'

Eliane's expression was still shuttered as she asked Sara, 'What did you do with the jacket?'

'I burned it on a bonfire.'

She gave a small nod of satisfaction. 'The best place for it. Those times are in the past now and it's best we look forwards, not backwards. Speaking of which, I'm delighted to see how much work you've done on the garden. I always think to plant a garden is to have faith in the future, don't you?'

Sara took this as a cue for the conversation to move on. 'I'll be pleased to show you round, and I'd love to hear more about how the gardens used to be laid out,' she smiled. 'I must warn you, though,' she went on apologetically, gesturing towards the photo of Eliane in her youth, 'I haven't had a chance to get to grips with the kitchen garden yet. That's a project for this winter. So you'll have to excuse the weeds there at present.'

'But I see the old pear tree's still there.' Eliane nodded to where the higher boughs, weighed down with their heavy gold fruit, were just visible above the weathered stone wall that enclosed the *potager*. 'That does my heart good.'

Sara passed Eliane the cup of herbal *tisane* that she'd asked for, and then poured tea for the rest of them. 'There are cartons of apple juice for Nathalie and Pierre if they'd like them,' she offered Gina.

'Perfect. But let's leave them where they are for the time being' – Gina was watching her children playing happily, Nathalie gently pushing Pierre on the baby swing and making him gurgle with laughter by clapping her hands in between pushes – 'and enjoy our peaceful cup of tea.'

Mireille picked up the bone-china cup carefully, her hands bent and knotted with arthritis. 'An occupational hazard,' she explained, flexing the stiffened fingers as she noticed Sara glance at them sympathetically. 'I worked as a seamstress, in the days before electric sewing machines.'

At last the children came back across the lawn, Pierre holding tightly to his big sister's hand as he toddled on slightly unsteady feet, and the old ladies' expressions brightened once more, the clouds of the past dispelled by the children's laughter and the sight of Pierre's eyes opening wide in delight at the prospect of a large slice of lemon drizzle cake.

'Let me show you what I've done in the gardens so far,' Sara offered Eliane, and they strolled through the grounds, Eliane nodding in approval as Sara explained her planting scheme, carefully planned to give continuous colour from spring to autumn as a backdrop for wedding photos. Mireille, leaning on her walking stick and Gina's arm, followed close behind.

Finally, they reached the viewpoint. 'Look.' Mireille nudged Eliane. 'You can see the old mill house from here.'

'Thomas told me there's a rumour that there's a secret tunnel running from the mill all the way up to the château,' Sara ventured. 'But I don't suppose it's true.'

Eliane's grey eyes fixed her with their gaze, suddenly as clear as a summer sky. '*Mais oui*, Sara, it is true. The tunnel itself is blocked off now though; it would be too dangerous to use these days. But it began and ended by opening out into a cavern at each end, most likely carved out by an ancient underground river before man walked the Earth. Remember, Mireille, we kept the pig in the cave down at the *moulin*?'

Sara remembered the stable door set into the rock face behind the mill. And then she felt a rising sense of excitement. 'And the cavern at the other end?'

'Why, my child, it's right here under our feet!' As Eliane's face broke into a broad smile, Sara caught a glimpse of the natural, breathtaking beauty of the nineteen-year-old girl she must have been, who'd worked here all those years ago. 'And the entrance to it is in your cellar, beneath the kitchen.'

She led the way back to the château and Sara handed her the key to the cellar door, flicking the light switch to illuminate the dark well of the stairs that led down to the wine store.

'Have you got a candle and some matches too? Bring them with us,' Eliane said.

'Pierre and I will stay here,' Mireille said firmly. 'We'll need to call out a search party if you get lost down there.'

'I've been down here hundreds of times and I've never seen anything,' Sara mused as they descended the cellar stairs. 'Maybe it's been filled in?'

As sure-footed as a teenager now, Eliane made her way past the racks of wine bottles, sleeping quietly in the cool darkness that helped to keep them in perfect condition until called upon to help animate the wedding celebrations above ground. She stooped under a low stone arch, into a smaller room in the shadows, away from the electric lights of the main cellar.

'The barrel store?' Sara asked.

'*Oui*.' Eliane struck a match and lit the candle. Her eyes glittered in the light of the small flame. 'The entrance is right here. Well hidden, *non*?'

132

Sara looked about her. The stone walls rose solidly on all sides, curving into a vaulted ceiling above their heads. Three big barrels, long ago emptied of the Bordeaux wines they once held, rested on their sides on the age-worn terracotta tiles of the floor in front of them. 'I can't see anything.'

'Look carefully.' Eliane bent low to hold the candle nearer floor level. 'Do you notice anything about the bases of the barrels?'

Sara looked more closely. Two of them had wooden chocks jammed in on each side to stop them from rolling out of position. But the third one had no chocks. Sara stepped back. Come to think of it, that one seemed to be sitting very slightly lower than the others, even though it was clearly the same size. She pointed towards the floor, hidden beneath the belly of the barrel.

'*Oui*, you've got it. The barrel sits on the opening. Here, take this.' Eliane handed the candle to Gina. 'Sara, give me a hand.'

They rolled the barrel sideways, and there, where it had lain, was a dark, rectangular hole leading even further down into the earth, rough stone steps just visible at the lip.

'Wow! The secret tunnel!' gasped Nathalie, gripping Gina's spare hand a little more tightly.

'Give me the candle and wait here.' Eliane's voice echoed slightly, bouncing off the vaulted ceiling. 'We need to make sure the air hasn't gone bad after being sealed up for so long.'

'Eliane, let me! Are you sure it's safe?' Sara peered down into the void as Eliane's white hair disappeared into the gloom. She turned to Gina. 'Wait here. I'll go in after her and make sure she's okay.'

Nathalie's eyes shone bright in the shadows of the barrel store, with a mixture of fear and excitement.

The steps descended steeply, almost vertical, but Sara could see the faint glow from the candle beneath her. Pressing her hands into the rough stone sides of the shaft, she felt her way downwards cautiously, the steps levelling out into a gently sloping tunnel just high enough for her to stand up in if she bowed her head. Suddenly, the claustrophobic space opened up before her and she found herself standing alongside Eliane. In the flickering glow of the candle's light, the white stone walls and roof of a sizeable cave were illuminated around them. The air was cool but surprisingly dry, with no hint of mustiness, despite having been sealed up for so long. Eliane turned to her, triumphant. '*Et voilà!*' she proclaimed, like a magician unveiling his very best trick.

'Oh, Eliane, it's incredible!' Sara gasped in amazement at this magical secret place that had been right there beneath her feet all this time.

Eliane seemed to be searching for something, holding the candle close to the stone. As the flame played across the smooth walls, excavated and shaped so many thousands of years ago by the flow of an ancient river, it suddenly picked out a shape, carved not by water but by the hand of man. A heart. With two sets of initials, set into the bedrock beneath the château. Eliane traced the shape with her fingertips, as if reading Braille, but in the candlelight her grey eyes shone once again with a light as clear as a summer's day.

'I wonder who they were.' Sara met Eliane's gaze. 'And when that heart was carved.'

Eliane smiled, her expression enigmatic. 'Your château is built on love, Sara. Love and happiness. No matter what sadness has happened here too. Always remember that.'

'Wow, that's amazing!' Gina and Nathalie crowded into the space behind them and the cloud fell over Eliane's expression again.

'We'd better not stay here too long. It needs a good airing after being shut up all these years.' Eliane held the candle away from the wall so that the carved heart faded back into the smooth stone once again. 'See over there,' she gestured. 'That's where the entrance to the tunnel used to be, that ran all the way down to the lower cave in the *moulin*.' An old opening at the far end of the cavern was blocked off with dense rubble, planks of wood fastened across it to hold the debris in place and stop it collapsing into the cave.

'Come, we'd better be going up now. Otherwise, Mireille and Pierre will be imagining we've disappeared into the centre of the Earth.' Eliane smiled reassuringly at Nathalie, who was still keeping a firm grip on Gina's hand.

They made their way back up, leaving the barrel rolled away from the entrance to the cave, although Sara took the precaution of piling a few boxes of wine in front of the gaping hole so that Antoine and Thomas couldn't step into it by accident. She couldn't wait to show them the château's secret and planned to come back here with a torch so that she could get a closer look at the initials carved into the cave wall. One set had looked like the letters E.M., though she couldn't be sure in the flickering of the candlelight.

She had a feeling there was another story here, one that involved Eliane's time at the château. She wanted to ask a thousand questions, curious to know what it had been like for each of the sisters as the hurricane of war had transformed their lives, one working here in this sleepy hamlet and the other embarking on her career as a seamstress in bustling Paris. But she understood now why a shadow had passed across the faces of Eliane and Mireille as they remembered those darker times, filled with fear and conflict. She respected their reticence and stayed quiet, allowing them to say only as much as they wanted, not pushing them through the doorways of memory that they'd rather keep closed. She hoped there'd be further visits in the future, when the sisters could tell her more . . .

Brushing off the dust and cobwebs from their clothes, they emerged, breathless and triumphant, into the sunny kitchen where Mireille and Pierre were waiting for them.

'*Maman!*' Pierre cried out, holding out his arms to Gina, relieved to see his mother and sister safely back again.

'Thank you so much for coming.' As they said their goodbyes, Sara held both Eliane's hands in hers. 'It's been lovely learning more about Château Bellevue. I'm so grateful to you for sharing your memories today.'

Eliane nodded and embraced Sara warmly. 'I'm glad it's in such good hands these days. We French don't like to think too much about the war years. But it's time some of these ghosts were laid to rest now.' She looked around at the roses against the stone of the château's walls, gently exuding their sweet scent into the late-afternoon air. 'A garden is a healing place. I'm sure we'll meet again before long.'

Then, fixing Sara again with that clear, calm gaze, Eliane said, 'At the end of a story we say, "*et ils vécurent heureux jusqu'à la fin de leurs jours*".'

Sara nodded. 'In English we would say, "and they all lived happily ever after".'

The old lady took Sara's hands in hers again for a moment, squeezing them as if to give her strength. 'I'm so pleased the château has found its rightful use in the end. Always remember, Sara, even in the darkest of times, love will light the way.'

Chapter 9

CHRISTA & BILL

Christa & Bill

*invite you to join them
for their wedding weekend.
From Thursday 30 August
Until Monday 3 September
At Château Bellevue de Coulliac*

'It's ironic, isn't it?' Karen remarked as she helped Sara arrange pretty bunches of flowers from the garden in an assortment of jugs and vases, one for each bedroom. 'Even though there are only twenty-four guests all told this time, it's still almost the same amount of work as for a hundred-odd.'

Sara nodded and stepped back to admire their handiwork. She'd collected this eclectic assortment of jars, bottles and jugs from markets and *brocantes* to use for filling the château with flowers and the effect was charming, in keeping with the simplicity of the country setting. At this stage in the season, the garden was in its final late-summer flush, the roses blooming one last time and clouds of pink and white cosmos helping to sustain the garden's beauty through the transition of the seasons.

'A couple more stems for the large vase should do it, I think.' She picked up her secateurs and went outside, fishing in her pocket for her mobile phone as it started to ring. Her hand trembled as she answered, noticing that the name of the bank was flashing up on the screen. Monsieur Dupuy, true to his word, was getting back to her before the week was out . . .

Their brief conversation over, she rang off and thrust the phone back into her pocket. Like a sleepwalker, she wandered over to the viewpoint and sat down on the bench.

Looking out at the view, it was as though everything was clearer than usual: the silver glint of the river brighter; the green of the vine-clad hillside more vibrant; the end-of-summer colours of the woodland leaves in the valley below softer.

Because now she was looking at it all through the lens of loss, already mentally taking a step back from one more thing that she'd loved but was going to have to relinquish. Her worst fears were realised: the answer from the bank was a *non*. The doors within her, which hope had dared to push ajar, slammed shut, and the stale taste of regret filled her mouth. She swallowed, with an effort, trying to find the strength that she'd had to tap into many times before in her life. And then, her energy drained, the heaviness of loss weighing down her heart, she hauled herself to her feet and made her way back to the kitchen. She'd just have to swallow her pride and contact Monsieur Bonneval, the estate agent. And hope that those buyers he'd mentioned hadn't bought anything else yet.

Karen looked at her sharply as she came through the door. 'Are you okay?'

'Yes, fine – why?'

'You went out to get some more flowers . . .'

Sara clutched her head and forced a rueful smile. 'Sorry, I'd forget my head these days if it wasn't screwed on.' Thankful for the distraction, she turned on her heel and strode back out into the garden, sternly telling herself yet again to get a grip. It was time to refocus on the weekend ahead.

◆ ◆ ◆

The château's corridors echoed with the sound of laughter and children's voices as the sprawling extended family settled in. The house party filled all the rooms, Bill and Christa's children and grandchildren spilling out of their bedrooms into the reception rooms and out to the garden.

'Sorry about the racket,' Bill apologised as Sara and Karen carried trays of tea and home baking on to the terrace. 'We're all a bit overexcited.'

'It's no problem at all,' Sara assured him. 'This place comes alive when it's filled with laughter. What a lovely lot of children!'

'Yes, we're guilty of doing our bit for world overpopulation, I'm afraid. We've three children each, and fourteen grandchildren to date . . . and counting,' he grinned, nodding fondly at a heavily pregnant daughter-in-law who was heading across the lawn in the direction of the swimming pool, holding a toddler firmly by the hand.

Christa sank down thankfully in an armchair. 'Tea, how lovely. After two days' drive, I must say that's a very welcome sight indeed. And cake too. Perfect.' She cut a slice of Victoria sponge, generously filled with jam and cream. 'Light as air,' she nodded approvingly. 'Did you bake this, Sara?'

'No, Karen's our cake expert.'

'Well, as I always say, you can never have too much cake.' Christa took a large bite and then licked the icing sugar off her fingers.

'A very sound philosophy indeed,' said Bill, accepting a piece.

'Some for you, dear?' Christa offered one of her willowy teenage granddaughters who was lounging on a sofa nearby.

The girl shuddered. 'No thank you, Granny. I don't do gluten. Or lactose. My body is a temple.'

Her grandmother peered at her over the top of her glasses. 'What utter nonsense. My body is more of a bus shelter, but I'm perfectly happy the way I am. Suit yourself, though – all the more for me.'

'Oh, all right then, since it *is* a special occasion.' The girl put down her glossy magazine. 'Just a tiny bit though . . .'

Sara glanced over her shoulder as she headed back to the kitchen, nudging Karen, who turned too, just in time to glimpse the girl tucking into a large slice of the cake.

'That was lovely, dear.' Christa brought her croissant-flecked plate over to the sink, where Sara and Hélène were starting to clear away the breakfast things. 'Such a treat for us all, having breakfast outside in the sunshine. And in September too – who'd have thought it!

Of course, some of the children should already be back in school, but I don't suppose it's going to damage their education too much, having a few extra days of summer to celebrate their old grandparents getting married. Some people' – she lowered her voice conspiratorially and nodded towards the terrace – 'think it's ridiculous at our age. I was all for carrying on living in sin, but Bill is such a romantic, he wanted to make an honest woman of me before we find ourselves knocking on the pearly gates and having to account to Saint Peter for our behaviour. I'm eighty-four years old, you know. I bet I'm the oldest bride you've ever had here?'

'Do you know, I think you are,' Sara smiled. 'So far, at least. It's wonderful!'

'So you don't think we're just a pair of old fools? Wasting our children's inheritance on a party like this?'

'Of course not. What could be nicer than an event that brings you all together to celebrate something so joyful? It must be lovely to have found companionship so late in life.'

'Why, yes, dear. And having sex again is pretty wonderful too, I can tell you. Fifteen years without is not so much a dry spell as a forced march across the Sahara Desert.'

Overhearing, Hélène nearly dropped the coffee pot she was drying.

'Granny! Granny! Will you come for a swim now? You promised you would after breakfast.' A swarm of assorted grandchildren invaded the kitchen.

'Of course, my darlings. Just let me go and get my costume on. No going near the pool until I get back now.' She fished a tissue out of her pocket and bent down to wipe the nose of one of the smaller boys, then sailed off, at a stately pace, to prepare to lead the poolside fun and games.

Hélène giggled. '*Quelle femme formidable!*' she whispered to Sara.

141

◆ ◆ ◆

'Right, you scurvy crew, here's how the treasure hunt works.' Bill had assembled all the grandchildren, and a couple of the younger ones' parents were joining in too, with Christa leading the pack for a treasure hunt he'd organised to keep the children out of their parents' hair on the morning of the wedding. 'Seven different caches of treasure have been hidden around the castle. You're going to have to work together as a team to solve each clue and find out where to look. I'll be sitting right here in the command centre, so each time you solve a clue you can come back to show me what you've found and I'll give you the next clue. The no-go areas are cordoned off with tape, as you can see, so I can promise you there's nothing hidden in the pool area or in the cottages beyond the walled garden. Some of the clues involve everyone in the team completing a sporting challenge before you can look for the treasure; others need a bit more brainpower. Everybody can help, from the youngest to the oldest' – and here he gave Christa a look. 'No exceptions. And no cheating' – and he gave Christa another look, at which she beamed angelically in reply. 'Any questions? Right then, here's your first clue.'

The treasure hunters streamed off across the lawn and could soon be seen running (or, in Christa's case, gliding serenely) to the viewpoint and back, each with a shuttlecock balanced on top of their head.

'Peace at last,' grinned Bill as he settled back in his deckchair to watch the fun. Karen and Sara were rolling cutlery in paper napkins in preparation for the buffet lunch that would be set out before everyone retired to their rooms to get dressed for the wedding party that afternoon.

'What a great idea,' Karen commented. 'I might just have to borrow it when we go to my sister's in Adelaide this Christmas.'

142

Ten minutes later there was an excited whoop. 'Uh-oh, brace yourselves, here they come again.' Bill fished the next clue out of his pocket as the hunt streamed back from the barn.

'Tiaras! Look, Grandpa, that treasure was tiaras!'

'Well done, it was indeed. Now, anyone who's a princess better put one on.' Bill handed them out, including the teenage granddaughters, who had temporarily forgotten how cool they were and put on their glitzy plastic crowns, giggling with as much enthusiasm as their smaller siblings.

'Aw! Grandpa, tiaras are for girls. The next treasure better be something for boys,' a small grandson complained.

'Well, you'd better solve the clue and see. Off you go!' Bill settled himself back in his chair as the treasure hunters swarmed off again.

The second batch of treasure turned out to be a stash of pirate hats, hanging from the branches of the old pear tree in the walled garden. One small granddaughter complained that she didn't want to wear a 'sissy Barbie tiara', but the well-prepared Bill had reckoned on such a mutiny and ordered in a couple of extra pirate hats. The spurned crown was swiftly redeployed so that, on the next foray, Sara smiled to see it sparkling gaily among Christa's grey curls.

'Found it!'

'But what *is* it?'

'It's a record, stupid!'

'What's a record?'

'It's sort of like a CD, only old-fashioned.'

'Does it play music?'

'Yes, but you need the right kind of machine to play it on.'

One of the younger children carried the single carefully back to Bill at the kitchen table.

'Grandpa, you should ask Father Christmas for a new phone. Then you can play lots of different music, not just one song.'

Sara and Karen exchanged an amused glance, enjoying watching the fun and games.

'Is it what I think it is?' asked Christa, reaching for her reading glasses. 'Oh, Bill, you old softie!'

He nodded. 'This, children, is not just any record. It's "Imagine" by the late, great John Lennon. And it just happens to be the record that I had my first slow dance to with Christa. So, in a sense, it's Our Song. We're going to dance to it at our wedding party later on. And it's most appropriate, because never did I "imagine" that I'd find so much love and so much happiness again at this time of life. It's a reminder to us all that we should always have hopes and dreams in life, otherwise how could we possibly even begin to start making them come true?'

The piratical granddaughter tugged at his sleeve. 'But Grandpa, we need the special machine.'

'Don't worry,' Sara smiled, 'we've got one. Thomas will play it for you.'

Christa bent down and kissed Bill tenderly.

'Eeew, sloppy stuff!' squirmed a small grandson.

'Yes, come on, Grandpa Bill, that's quite enough of that,' one of the teenagers chipped in. 'What about the next clue?'

Red, white and blue streamers were unearthed next, and then a sizeable cache of confetti and a basketful of sugared almonds.

'I'll look after all of these. They'll come in handy later.' Bill firmly shooed the children away from the table. 'Oh well, all right then, three sweets each, just to keep you going.'

'Hey! Granny Christa took four.'

'The prerogative of my age, my darling. And anyway, with all this dashing about the place, a bride has to keep her strength up,' said Christa unapologetically.

'Now,' said Bill, 'another clue. See if you can work it out. Then bring whatever you find back to me and I'll give you the very last clue, to find the greatest treasure of all.'

'It says there's gold buried in a deep, dark dungeon. Cool! Does this castle have dungeons, Sara?'

She nodded solemnly. 'That door over there leads down to the cellars. Thomas here has got the key and he's going to take you down there, on condition that you go very, very carefully. And that you don't touch any of the wine! Make sure you stick together because we've lost the occasional guest down there, never to be seen again. And you never know, you may even find the secret passageway that's rumoured to be down there. Here,' she said, handing out torches to the little ones, 'you'll need these to see where you're going.'

Bill winked at her as the cellar stairs swallowed up the treasure hunters. 'Thanks for getting into the swing of all this, Sara. You're a good sport.'

'It's no problem, Bill. I'm enjoying it as much as they all are. And I'm looking forward to finding out what the greatest treasure of all might be.'

A few minutes later they re-emerged from the cellar, a little dustier than when they'd gone down and some of the pirate hats were now festooned with a spiderweb or two.

'We found it! Sara, we found the secret tunnel! And there was a cave! With the treasure in it.'

'It really was buried treasure this time! Look, Grandpa!'

The children brandished a small jeweller's box and sitting on the velvet within were two gold wedding bands.

'Well, that's lucky! We wouldn't have been able to get married without the rings,' Bill exclaimed. 'Right then, let's see what we've got. Who's got nice neat handwriting? Okay, take this paper and pencil and write down all the treasures you've found so far. So it was tiaras, hats, "Imagine", streamers, confetti, almonds, rings. Now, here's the final clue.' He handed it over.

'It says, "The greatest treasure of all can be found by rearranging the first letters of each of the items you've found.""

With the tip of her tongue protruding from the corner of her mouth, Christa's youngest granddaughter carefully wrote out, 'T . . . h . . . i . . . s . . . c . . . a . . . r . . .'

'This car! The greatest treasure of all is a car!' shouted a small grandson.

'No, you dummy, we've got to rearrange the letters to make another word. It's a puzzle.'

They pored over the piece of paper.

'T-chairs!'

'What on earth are t-chairs?'

'No, wait! I've got it!'

'Me too! Me too!'

'Granny Christa, it's you! The greatest treasure of all is you.'

'Well done, all of you. You've cracked it!' He ruffled his grandson's hair. 'Love is the most important thing there is, at any age.' He hugged his bride to him, gently brushing a cobweb from the plastic tiara that sat, slightly skew-whiff, on her grey curls. 'Now, let's clear out of here and go and have a swim. Your parents have had far too much peace and quiet, and we need to leave Sara and her team to set out the lunch.' He clapped his hands to shoo the children through the door and out into the sunshine beyond. 'We're on a tight schedule, after all: don't you know we've got a wedding to go to this afternoon!'

◆ ◆ ◆

Sara lay with her head pillowed in the dip between Thomas's shoulder and his chest, where it seemed to fit so perfectly, like a piece of a jigsaw slotting into place. The post-wedding party had finished a little earlier than usual and they'd left the last few guests content-edly sipping nightcaps on the terrace under the stars.

'What?' Sara gazed at Thomas's profile as he lay smiling up at the ceiling.

He turned his head to look into her eyes. 'A great day, that's all. I liked that old couple a lot.' Sorrow clouded the expression in his eyes. 'Selling this place is going to be terrible. Not just for you, but for all of us.'

Sara smiled sadly back at him. 'I know. I'll have to call Monsieur Bonneval, but I'm not going to do it until after our final wedding of the season. I want to have one more week of simply being here. I can't bear to think about it. Losing the château. And today made me realise that you've all become a family to me – Karen, Antoine, the Héls Belles . . . I guess it was seeing Bill and Christa and their whole sprawling collection of children and grandchildren. It was a great reason for a party. It may even have restored my faith in weddings!'

Thomas nodded, remembering. 'Did you see their grandchil-dren all wore their pirate hats and tiaras for the ceremony? I think that littlest girl is probably sleeping in hers!'

'I know. And they loved going into the secret cave. Do you think they disturbed the ghosts there?'

'Sure to have,' he smiled. 'But that's the best way to lay ghosts to rest: with happiness and laughter.'

'So do you believe ghosts really can be exorcised?'

'Eventually.' His eyes were serious as they gazed into hers. 'Some take longer than others, but with enough love they all leave in the end.' He brushed a strand of hair from her cheek so tenderly that she knew he wasn't talking about the castle's ghosts any more, but her own personal demons. And as they moved together and his lips met hers, she even believed, in that moment, that what he said was true.

Chapter 10

A Proposal

Peace reigned over the château once again.

Sara finished her lunch of leftovers from the Sunday evening supper and sauntered out into the garden. It was a stunning autumn afternoon, the sky the pure, delicate blue of a robin's egg and not a cloud anywhere in sight. The edge had been taken off the summer's heat now, and the September sunlight had a ripe softness to it, turning the stone walls of the château the same mellow colour as the sweet white wine that Thomas's family would soon be pressing from the grapes at Château de la Chapelle.

He'd gone back there this morning, having said goodbye to Bill and Christa and waved their sprawling family off down the drive.

'Papa says he wants to see me,' he'd grumbled. 'I wanted to have lunch with you, just the two of us in peace and quiet. But he's insisted I go home to join him and Robert. Must be to discuss the plans for the harvest, I suppose. Although I don't know why we have to do it today, when there's still at least a fortnight to go before we begin,' he'd sighed.

'Never mind,' she'd replied. 'I'll make us something delicious for supper tonight. Just the two of us and a bottle of wine on the terrace . . .' She'd broken off, overcome by the urge to kiss his lips, which were spreading wide in that familiar slow, sleepy smile as his eyes met hers.

She picked up a wicker basket that sat on the step at the kitchen door and wandered into the walled garden to collect the windfall pears that were carpeting the ground beneath the old tree. Wasps wove drunkenly through the branches, sating themselves on the sweet, ripe fruit that hung heavy above her head. A faint smell of fermentation rose up from the pears at her feet, some of which were already softening and rotting where they'd fallen. She chose the least bruised of the fruit and had soon gathered a generous basketful.

The afternoon's heady warmth was soporific and so she sat down on the makeshift bench that they'd built alongside the pear tree, comprising a length of an old beam balanced on two large cornerstones, propped against the wall that enclosed the garden. The basket of pears at her feet, she leaned her head back against the lichen-spotted wall, tilting her face to the sun's mellow warmth and closing her eyes drowsily, just for a few moments . . .

She must have dropped off because the next thing she knew, Thomas was waking her with a gentle kiss.

'Hey there, Sleeping Beauty. You look so peaceful. I hardly wanted to wake you, but I have news and I need to tell you straight away!' His eyes shone, his expression alive with suppressed excitement. He sat down beside her on the bench and took her hand in his.

'We had a family conference over lunch, and I have a proposition to put to you,' he began. 'But where to begin . . . ? Okay, first I have to explain something about French law to you. You see, under the Code Napoléon, inheritance laws here mean that each child in a family automatically inherits an equal share of any estate. This means that when my father dies, Robert and I will each have an equal share of Château de la Chapelle. But it also creates a problem, as our children and our children's children will also each be entitled to an equal share, so the vineyard would be subdivided into smaller and smaller parts and end up not being economically viable. And that's leaving aside the fact that everyone might not be in agreement about how it should be run, who should live where, and so on. Papa has seen this coming for some time. So the reason he called Robert and me there for lunch today was to propose a solution. He has been quietly saving up enough capital over the years to be able to give one of us the farm and the other an equivalent amount of money to go and set up somewhere else. He now believes the time is right, in the lives of both his sons, to hand over to us. He wanted us to decide between ourselves who would have the vineyard and who would move on, but of course the answer is obvious. Robert is devoted to the vineyard and I don't have that same level of attachment.'

Sara squeezed his hand, trying to feel pleased about his newly found freedom and to push away the awful thought that now he would have the means to leave. 'Oh, Thomas, that's wonderful. Your dream has come true!'

'Yes,' he nodded. 'And now that it has, I find that in fact my dream has changed a little. You see, I've fallen under the spell of a beautiful enchantress and she's opened my eyes to the richness of the world right here in my own backyard. The web that she spins, here in her hilltop castle, draws in people from near and far. I've had the best summer of my life with you, Sara, meeting so many people from different places and different backgrounds, seeing such different ways they have of celebrating their love. You've even taught me a thing or two about the history of my own corner of the world that I didn't know before. And, most of all, you've woven your web around my heart and now I don't want to leave.'

He paused to kiss her.

'So my proposition – which is purely a business one, you understand – is this: I would like to invest in Château Bellevue and become your business partner.'

He held up a hand to stop her as she started to protest. 'My father, who is my best and most shrewd advisor on such matters, is as impressed as anyone with the work you've done here, and he thoroughly approves of your plans for the future. He would love it if I could be involved. I don't have the money to buy out the whole of Gavin's share – and anyway, Papa said that you probably wouldn't want to get yourself back into that situation after what's happened. So I'm proposing to buy thirty per cent of the business. That way, we can take out a bank loan for the rest of the money you need to pay off Gavin, and you will become the majority shareholder.'

Sara began to protest again. Despite what he'd said, alarm bells were going off in her head at the thought that, if Thomas owned a share of the business, she might just be getting herself back into the same position she'd been in before. Panic rose in her at the idea that she'd lose control of what she'd worked so hard to create; that she'd risk losing the sense of self-confidence she'd clawed back following Gavin's departure; that if Thomas were to get involved on a formal basis in the business then it might warp and distort their relationship.

She pulled herself up short. She wasn't going to lose her voice again now that she'd found it at last. She swallowed down the reflex rejection – her default protective response – that was forming itself in her throat, and then calmly and clearly told him her fears.

Thomas heard her out, listening carefully, watching her face as she spoke. 'I know, I know, and I understand you, Sara. But nothing will change between us. We'll get it all drawn up legally so that you can rest assured you will always have control over your own destiny. Papa told me he can see that's important to you. He told me I should set you free, economically speaking, because then we will both know that if you choose to stay here in France it's because this is where you really want to be. As the majority shareholder, you will still be the Boss. And we've already proven this summer that we can work well together on that basis. Don't worry – I think my male ego can take it.' His slow, easy smile proved his point.

'But your dreams of travelling the world . . . I don't want to be the one who stops you.'

He nodded. 'I know. I still want to go to so many places. I thought maybe, if we worked very hard in the summer, we could go away together sometimes in the winter months. I think I will enjoy my adventures abroad even more if you are part of them. Would you travel with me, if you knew you always had your home here to come back to?'

Sara nodded slowly, then sat stunned, thankful to feel the solid reassurance of the stone wall at her back or, she thought, she might have collapsed with the sense of confusion and relief that was making her head spin. As she considered Thomas's proposition from every angle, her heart beat faster and a sense of joy began to percolate through her veins, matching the joy that was written before her on the face of the man she loved.

'But Robert . . . ?'

'He's delighted too. He'll take over the vineyard. Of course, I'll go and lend a hand whenever he needs me, but Gina can take on the whole of the marketing side. And Robert's thinking of offering Antoine a position in the wine cellar: it will help him to gain some work experience, which he needs to do as part of his university course. There might even be a permanent job for him there when he's finished. And Christine is thrilled as they're going to move into the main house with the children, so the boys won't have to share a bedroom any more. Papa will move into their house . . .' He tailed off, and a pregnant pause hung in the air between them.

'And you will move in here with me?' Sara's heart skipped a beat with nervous hope.

'If you'll have me. You are the boss, after all.'

Her kiss told him all he needed to know.

They sat a while longer, making plans, discussing ideas, thinking of new ways to promote the business, the golden afternoon stretching itself out into a future filled with promise.

At last, when the shadows began to reach their dark fingers across the rough, weed-filled grass towards where they sat, they got to their feet.

'Here, let me take that.' Thomas picked up the basket of pears and they strolled back towards the château. Still deep in conversation, immersed in their plans for the future, he absent-mindedly picked up one of the golden fruits and took a bite.

'We can make the walled garden into a really beautiful vegetable patch,' Sara was saying. 'I'd like to get Eliane back to advise me on what to plant . . .' And then, 'Thomas? *Thomas!* she screamed.

For he had fallen silent, his eyes widening in a reflexive mask of fear. He opened his mouth to choke out the chunk of pear he'd bitten off and on it crawled a wasp, woozy with sweet juice and having just discharged its sting deep into the soft tissues of Thomas's throat.

The effect happened so fast that Sara scarcely had time to think. He dropped the basket, pears spilling across the grass at their feet, and sank to his knees, his hands clutching at his throat as if to try and pull out the poison. Within moments, his neck and jawline were swelling alarmingly and his eyes dilated with panic.

'Thomas! Speak to me! What can I do? Can you talk?'

He gasped something she couldn't make out, his tongue swollen into the roof of his mouth now.

'*Help!* Sara screamed. 'Someone help me!'

Antoine and Héloise appeared at a run. 'Oh, thank God!' cried Sara. 'Call an ambulance, quick!'

'You phone the paramedics,' Antoine shouted to Héloise. '*Je vais chercher son auto-injecteur dans la voiture.*'

It must only have been a minute or two before Antoine reappeared with a small plastic box, but by now Thomas was lying on the ground, gasping for the breaths that were becoming more and more forced. Sara cradled his head in her lap, desperately trying to make her voice sound calm as she reassured him that help was on the way. Antoine handed the box to her and she opened it to find two EpiPens, each containing the life-saving dose of adrenaline that those with severe allergies carry with them wherever they go. A miracle! Sara realised Antoine must have seen them in Thomas's van at some point, thank heavens.

'I don't know what to do!' She was struggling to hold back the panic now. 'Thomas, listen to me. Where do we inject this?'

He gesticulated towards his leg, his eyes transformed to slits in the puffy skin of his face.

Without time to give it a second thought, she ripped the injector from its packet, pulled off the safety cap and pressed the tip firmly into his thigh, the plunger driving down to release its dose into his bloodstream. She held her breath, willing the terrifying rasp of his breathing to ease a little.

'They're on their way,' shouted Héloise, reappearing at a run.

Thomas's eyes locked on to Sara's, widening with fear as his features lost definition within his ballooning face.

'It's going to be okay,' she told him. 'The ambulance is on its way. Hold on, just a few minutes more.'

But his breaths had now become short gasps, his chest heaving as his body desperately tried to take in air.

'Quick, Antoine! The other syringe!' Sara had no idea whether it was safe to administer more adrenaline, but she knew she only had a split second to make the decision. She plunged the second dose into his thigh.

'Don't you dare leave me, Thomas Cortini,' she whispered, bending her lips to his ear.

He heard her. His eyes widened again for a moment and she felt a surge of relief as his expression softened suddenly into one of such complete love and acceptance that it made her want to cry. She stroked his hair and bent to kiss him, just as they heard the faint wail of a siren and Héloise shouted, 'They're here, I can see the lights!'

But then Thomas's eyes rolled back in his head and, with a final rasping gasp, his breathing stopped.

◆ ◆ ◆

The little hospital in Sainte-Foy-la-Grande was a warren of vinyl-floored corridors and Sara's shoes squeaked faintly as she followed the nurse, stopping before a closed door. 'It's okay, you can go in,' the nurse said.

She pushed the door open cautiously, not sure whether Thomas would be awake. He lay still between the crisp white sheets, a tangle of wires hitched up from his body to the steadily beeping monitor beside him, his face obscured by a plastic mask that hissed quietly as it fed his lungs with life-giving oxygen. She tiptoed to his bedside, relieved to see the trace on the monitor zigzagging its way across the screen in a steady pulse.

In those awful moments after his breathing had stopped, the paramedics had managed to get a breathing tube down his throat to reopen the airway. 'How much adrenaline has he had?' they'd demanded as they worked quickly and deftly, listening for his heartbeat. She'd showed them the two empty EpiPens. '*Bon,*' they'd nodded. 'His heart hasn't stopped. You did the right thing.' They'd administered more injections and then, with a miraculous gasp, his chest had risen as he took a breath, making Sara's own heart convulse as she gave an involuntary sob of relief. 'His blood pressure's still dangerously low. We need to get him to hospital straight away.' The medics had eased Thomas's prone body on to a stretcher and quickly lifted it into the ambulance.

Very gently, one of the men had put a restraining hand on Sara's arm as she made to climb in after it. 'I'm sorry,' he'd said. 'I may need to work on him *en route*. There won't be room for you.' He'd turned to Antoine. 'Can you bring her to Sainte-Foy? We'll be able to update you when you get there. And you'd better call his family as well.'

'Of course.' Sara dialled Patrick Cortini, but when he answered the phone and she opened her mouth to explain, she found she could get no words out and tears began to pour uncontrollably down her face. Antoine, who was standing beside her, gently took the phone from her shaking hand and spoke to Thomas's father, his voice calmly relaying the urgency of the situation. He hung up the call and then, putting an arm round Sara's shoulders, he led her to the car that Héloïse had arrived in. 'Come. We'll take you.'

She had no memory of the drive to Sainte-Foy along twisting country roads. All she could remember was how she'd strained to catch a glimpse of the flashing lights of the ambulance on the road ahead but seen nothing; that, and the way her heart had seemed too big for her chest as it pounded with her love for Thomas and her terror that she might lose him.

They'd been shown to the waiting room on arrival at the hospital, the stretcher with Thomas's still-unconscious body having been whisked straight into an emergency room where the door was firmly shut. 'We'll let you know as soon as we have news,' the nurse had said, giving nothing away, although the expression in her eyes was grave behind her professionally sympathetic smile. Patrick and Robert arrived a few minutes later and Patrick embraced Sara in his strong arms, smoothing her hair as she wept on his shoulder. 'I'm so sorry,' she'd whispered.

'You, above all others, have nothing to be sorry for,' he told her. And those were all the words that were possible as they sat side by side on the hard, grey plastic chairs, holding hands tightly, waiting to hear whether Thomas would live.

After what seemed like an eternity, during which Sara willed Thomas back to life with each breath she took, a nurse finally appeared in the doorway. She smiled broadly and nodded. 'He's come round. He's going to be all right.'

The waiting room erupted with cries of thanksgiving and relief, as all five of the anxious watchers hugged each other and wept with joy.

'You can come and see him. But one at a time.' The nurse held up a finger to stop the stampede.

Sara stood back to let Patrick go first, but he shook his head. 'My boy has just had a near-death experience. Let him see the face he really wants to see the most. I think he deserves a truly beautiful welcome back to the land of the living!'

She stood at Thomas's bedside. His face was almost unrecognisable, swollen and blotchy, the lower half covered by the plastic oxygen mask. His hand rested at his side, the brown, work-toughened fingers looking helpless and vulnerable against the cold white sheet. Hesitantly, she reached out to touch them. His eyes opened, still lost in the puffiness of the surrounding skin. The green pulse on the heart monitor seemed to pick up its pace a little, the beep giving away his body's response to her touch. She bent to kiss his forehead tenderly, her tears of joy anointing his hair, and the two of them stayed that way for a few moments, the silence broken only by the quiet background hiss from the oxygen cylinder and the steadily reassuring electronic murmur of the monitor.

Drawing back a little, she stroked his poor face with gentle compassion. He reached up a hand and pulled the oxygen mask away from his mouth.

She put out a hand to restrain him. 'Don't you need that?'

'Not now that you're here.' His swollen tongue still made his speech a little indistinct. 'Sorry I gave you such a scare. And I really don't think I'm looking at my best right now.'

She looked at him, narrowing her eyes mock critically. 'Well, you do look a bit like Shrek, now you come to mention it. Just a little less green, perhaps,' she laughed. 'But I quite like this look on you. In fact, I could probably even learn to love it, if you're thinking of making a habit of eating wasps.'

He smiled. 'Wonderful. You've passed the test. Now I know you truly love me for who I am, not just for my amazing good looks!'

She came round to the other side of the bed, carefully avoiding the wires hooking him up to the machines at his side. 'Move over,' she nudged him, and climbed on to the bed to lie beside him so that she could hold him in her arms and feel his around her in return. He pulled the oxygen mask right down so that he could kiss her properly. 'Weird,' he said. 'I can't feel a thing.' Then he kissed her again. 'Wow. Pins and needles in my lips. I think you're bringing me back to life.'

Just then there was a cautious tap on the door and Patrick's head appeared round it. He beamed when he caught sight of the two of them. 'That's my boy,' he said approvingly. 'Great to see you're in such good hands!'

Thomas reached out his free hand and held on to his father's tightly. Sara gently pulled the oxygen mask back into place and got up from the bed, kissing Patrick on the cheek as she passed, going out to give the two of them some time together and to report back to Robert and the others in the waiting room. Her heartbeat was still a little unsteady, she noticed, as her shoes squeaked down the corridor, but now, rather than pounding in terror, it was because it was skipping and racing with the sheer joy of Thomas being alive: *joie de vivre*.

Chapter 11

PIPPA & JOSH

Mr David Hall
and
Mr and Mrs Henry Cavendish

request the pleasure of your company at the marriage of

Philippa Hall

to

Captain Joshua Cavendish

At Château Bellevue de Coulliac
on Saturday 8th September
at 3.30 p.m.

RSVP
Mrs Henry Cavendish
120 Eaton Square
London SW1W 9BE

'Okay, team, last wedding of the season. Let's make sure it's as good as all the others have been. Antoine, we're going to need a hand swapping the beds over. We'll be turning the garden room into the honeymoon suite this time round. The groom is disabled so they need wheelchair access.'

'I can help,' said Thomas. He was sitting at the kitchen table with them, having been released from hospital the previous evening. His face had shrunk back almost to its usual size, just a little puffiness remaining in his lips. 'I look just like a celebrity now,' he'd remarked last night, pouting like a Hollywood starlet into the mirror as he brushed his teeth in the cottage.

Sara dug him in the ribs. 'Don't be so vain! You remind me of a goldfish I had when I was little,' she laughed, bringing him back down to earth with a bump. She couldn't stop hugging him, touching him at every opportunity, to reassure herself of his warm, solid presence.

She turned to him now. 'Thomas, leave it to us. You need to rest after all you've been through. Save your strength for Saturday night.'

'Nonsense,' he protested. 'They pumped me so full of adrenaline and steroids at the hospital that I'm now super-human.'

He stood up and then immediately sat down again as his legs wobbled beneath him and his head spun.

'Watch yourself, Tommy-boy.' Karen ruffled his hair fondly as she passed. 'You're still more Rubber-Man than Superman. You can direct operations from here today. Leave it to us.' She turned to Sara. 'I'll get the Allen keys.'

As they worked to transform the ground-floor guest bedroom into a space worthy of the bridal couple, Sara briefed Karen and the Héls Belles. 'The groom is an ex-serviceman, injured on duty in Afghanistan. Lost the use of his legs, poor man. He's marrying his physiotherapist – they met while he was in rehab.'

'Oh, that's *so* romantic,' sighed Hélène. 'A handsome soldier and a beautiful therapist.'

'Hmm, well, from what I can gather there's a bit more to it than that. His mother seems to be most disapproving about this marriage. Apparently, he was originally engaged to be married to what she calls "a most suitable gel", but after he was injured the suitable gel decided not to go through with it. I feel a bit sorry for the new bride, who is going to have a disapproving battleaxe of a mother-in-law to contend with. Mrs Cavendish told me, when she phoned to confirm the booking here, that they'd had the original wedding all planned in the regimental chapel. But when it fell through, everything had to be cancelled, of course. And then her son announced he'd fallen in love with what she calls "the nurse" and they refused to have the service in England. Felt they wanted to get away somewhere that had no associations with the previous plans, I suppose, understandably. But Mrs Cavendish is in despair as she says she knows nothing about Pippa's "people" – as she puts it, at frequent intervals.'

'What a snob,' sniffed Karen.

'Now, now. It's not our place to judge. Although I have to confess she did put my back up when she said she was going to have to make all the arrangements as Pippa's family is almost non-existent. "No pedigree" was the exact phrase she used.'

'Well, then, it's a good job it's a wedding, and not Crufts,' Karen retorted tartly.

Héloise chipped in, as she and Antoine dismantled the twin beds, 'If they're in love then that's all that counts.'

'And anyway, I reckon it's better to be a mongrel than a bitch!' was Karen's searing parting shot as she headed upstairs to start on the other rooms.

'Right, you lot, that's enough of the scurrilous gossip. We're here to make this a happy and memorable day for everyone involved. It's the bride's day, but her in-laws are footing the bill, so let's do our best to help them all enjoy it.'

◆ ◆ ◆

The bride's expression was not exactly one of joyous anticipation. In fact, Sara could sense waves of anxiety and anguish flash across her face as she went out to greet Pippa and Josh. Josh was stroking his bride's hand, trying to reassure her. 'Don't worry, it'll turn up in time. The airline said they'll make sure they get it on another flight, so it'll easily be here later.' He turned in his wheelchair to shake hands with Sara and Thomas. 'Bit of a drama with the luggage, I'm afraid. The most important suitcase got left behind at Gatwick. Wedding dress, the whole bang-shoot.'

The bride smiled. She was trying to put a brave face on it but her lower lip was looking a little wobbly. 'All I've got is my wedding shoes and my underwear. At least I had *them* in my hand baggage.'

'Sounds all right to me!' Josh tried to cheer her up. 'Just wear those and we'll be fine.'

'Oh, you poor girl.' Sara couldn't help but give Pippa a reassuring hug. 'That's the last thing you need at this stage in the proceedings. Which airline was it?'

'Well, that's the irony,' said Pippa. 'We booked all the flights with the same airline, to come here and then onwards for the honeymoon. It was more expensive that way, but we thought it'd be safer. We'd have been better off on one of the cheaper ones probably. But they have reassured us it'll be here later today.'

'I can drive to Bordeaux airport to collect it if you like,' offered Thomas. 'That way it'll be one less thing for you to worry about.'

'Oh, that's so kind – would you?' When she smiled, there was a flash of the radiance they'd come to expect in their brides. Pippa's tense shoulders seemed to relax just a little.

'Of course – all part of the service. Now, come and let us show you the château and your room.' Sara led the way, with Pippa pushing the wheelchair and Antoine bringing up the rear, carrying the bags that had made it.

The couple had arrived before any of the other guests, including the dreaded Mrs Cavendish. Sara was pleased that this gave the pair a chance to see round their wedding venue in their own time and enjoy a few hours together peacefully before the onslaught began and Pippa's new mother-in-law waded into the fray.

After they'd settled into their room she gave them a tour of the chapel, the dining marquee and the barn where the reception would be held, and then installed them in the sunshine on the terrace with a restorative afternoon tea. They looked so happy together, just the two of them. She suspected that the wedding was going to be quite an ordeal for Pippa, being scrutinised and judged.

From the kitchen window, Sara could see a convoy of hire cars winding its way up the driveway from the road below. She dried her hands on a tea towel and went out to the car park. A large, immaculately coiffed lady in an expensive-looking lilac jacket was commanding her husband to 'Mind that hatbox, Henry! I'm not going to be able to find another Belinda Foster anywhere around here if you damage it . . .', thereby ensuring that anyone who was listening was aware that she had invested some serious money in her outfit in order to outdo everybody else in the wedding party.

'Mrs Cavendish?' Sara proffered a hand. 'Welcome to Château Bellevue de Coulliac.'

◆ ◆ ◆

Having safely installed the guests in their rooms, Sara headed to the kitchen to check the preparations for dinner were coming along smoothly. She glanced repeatedly at her phone. She was expecting a text from Thomas to confirm that he'd picked up Pippa's suitcase safely at Bordeaux airport and was on his way back with it. They both knew the bride would only be able to relax – in so far as that was going to be a possibility – once she knew it was safely on its way to the château . . . The phone rang and Sara snatched it up. 'Have you got it? What? What! What the hell did they go and do that for?' Her voice rose before she could stop herself, and she quickly pulled herself together as Héloïse and Hélène looked up from where they were prepping the vegetables for that night's dinner, looking at her wide-eyed. 'But how quickly can they get it back? Is there nothing they can do? Tell them to turn the plane around!' she remonstrated into the phone. 'Okay . . . okay. I'll go and tell her. See you back here soon.'

Sara rang off. The Héls Belles were looking at her expectantly as she stood in silence for a few seconds. She took a deep breath. 'Well, I'd better go and tell Pippa that her suitcase is going to be waiting for her when she arrives in Mauritius for her honeymoon. They've gone and put it on the wrong flight. Someone at the airline found their booking for the flight on Sunday and assumed that was where it was to go . . . so we have a bride who is about to have to face the mother-in-law from hell and a daunting crowd of socially aware wedding guests, with no wedding dress.'

She raked her fingers through her hair in exasperation. Poor Pippa was going to be devastated. And Mrs Cavendish would certainly make the most of this ghastly situation, milking it for all it was worth. What on earth could they do? It was already Friday afternoon, less than twenty-four hours to go to the wedding. And here, in the depths of rural France, designer wedding dress emporia were somewhat few and far between.

Hélène and Héloïse exchanged a glance and Héloïse nodded.

'What size would you say she is?' asked Hélène.

'Oh, a bit smaller than me, I think. A ten at most. Probably an eight. English sizes, I mean.'

'There may be something we can do.' Hélène scrolled through the contacts on her own phone.

'Anything!' Sara exclaimed. 'Although what we probably need right now is a miracle . . .'

◆ ◆ ◆

She tapped tentatively on the door of the makeshift honeymoon suite. 'Come in!' called Josh. He was lying on the bed and Pippa was massaging his legs. 'See how wonderful my lovely bride is?' he said cheerfully. 'She even keeps the circulation going for her useless husband. So beautiful and so talented in very many departments. I know I'm the luckiest man alive. One of these days I'm determined I'm going to stand on my own two feet again, with her help.'

Sara felt a slight catch in her throat and was unsure whether it was down to her nerves at what she now had to tell Pippa or the sight of this touchingly brave couple, who would certainly face challenges in their future together but who were so happy to be facing them together. Over the course of this season, she'd been able to observe a fair range of couples up close and personal, the emotional pressure cooker of a wedding always a good test of a relationship, but here, surely, was the definition of true love.

'Any word from Thomas yet?' asked Pippa.

'Actually, there is. And I think you'd better sit down . . .'

The blood drained from Pippa's face as Sara began to explain.

◆ ◆ ◆

'Turn right here.' Hélène leaned through the gap between the front seats of the car and directed Sara past the *mairie* in the hamlet of

Saint André-et-Appelles and up the hill through vines and plum trees. Turning into a small country lane, Hélène pointed out Gina and Cédric's house, where a large black cat sat basking in the afternoon sunshine like a furry Buddha. A little further on they pulled up in front of a stone cottage, where a tiny old lady dressed in black and leaning on a walking stick stood waiting for them in the doorway.

The four of them – Hélène and Héloise, Sara and Pippa – clambered out of the car. 'Mireille, it's so good to see you again,' Sara said, kissing her warmly on each cheek.

Héloise made the introductions. '*Mamie, je te présente Pippa Hall.*'

Sara felt a pang of doubt as the old lady led the way into her house. The girls had said she had a dress that might just fit Pippa, but were they really going to find something suitable here? *Well, beggars can't be choosers*, thought Sara, and then winced at the phrase: Mrs Cavendish already thought her daughter-in-law was exactly that. They were going to have to work a miracle, under these dire circumstances, to prove her wrong.

Mireille led them up a steep and narrow flight of stairs, her stick thudding on the floorboards, to an attic bedroom under the eaves of the stone house. Hanging on the door of a vast mahogany *armoire* was a white linen sheet, pinned at the bottom to shroud the dress. The girls bent to undo the pins and a little cloud of dried lavender flowers tumbled out on to the wide wooden floorboards, releasing their dusty fragrance into the early evening sunlight that streamed in through the open window. Carefully, reverentially, they eased the sheet off, under their grandmother's direction.

Sara gasped. And then turned to look at Pippa, who stood gazing at the dress, dumbfounded. Mireille's eyes sparkled, clearly delighted at their reaction. She stroked the soft cream silk, her gnarled, arthritic fingers gentle against the delicate fabric.

'I've never seen anything so beautiful!' said Pippa, looking as if she might burst into tears at any moment.

'This is incredible,' said Sara. 'It looks like . . .' She tailed off.

Hélène nodded. 'It's Christian Dior. The New Look. Vintage 1947.'

Mireille spoke in rapid-fire French and Héloise translated for Pippa's benefit.

'My grandmother was a seamstress, working in Paris for a small – and then relatively unknown – *couturier* when she met my grandfather, who was fighting for the Free French during the war. They got married once the war was over and came back to live down here. She made her wedding dress, with a little help from the *couturier* himself. It's made out of parachute silk, because it was hard to come by other fabrics for wedding dresses at that time, but you can see they embroidered it with silk thread and sewed on these seed pearls, which Monsieur Dior himself provided.'

'It's the New Look style,' continued Hélène. 'See how the waist is nipped in but the skirt is so full. It was Dior's reaction to the end of rationing, a statement of plenty after the tight skirts of the war years.'

Mireille added something else in scornful tones and the girls giggled.

'Mamie says it was also a reaction against Mademoiselle Coco Chanel. Those tight little suits were her signature style but she didn't exactly make herself popular in Paris during the war. She had an affair with one of the Nazis and took herself off to Switzerland to escape the scandal and disapproval. Dior's new style was a real statement that it was the beginning of a new era for France, in many different ways.'

The old lady reached out a claw-like hand to Pippa and ushered her forward.

'Well,' said Sara, 'you'd better try it on.'

167

In the golden light laden with dust motes and scented faintly with lavender and cedar-wood, Pippa stood before them in The Dress. It fitted her like a glove. Her tiny waist was accentuated by the circular skirt, which hung beautifully from her slender hips, its full underskirt making it flare elegantly just above her ankles. The bodice of the dress, lovingly hand-embroidered with flowers whose stamens were picked out in tiny pearls, enhanced her slim figure, and the deep V-neckline drew the eye to her pretty face.

'*Voilà!*' said Mireille with satisfaction, as she gently tugged a last fold of the skirt into place. '*Une vraie princesse.*'

Pippa turned to gaze into the misty depths of an old *cheval* mirror, her four handmaidens clustered behind her, and a sob burst from her as she saw her reflection. Through her tears, she smiled at Mireille and reached out to hold both of the old lady's wrinkled hands in her own. 'How can I ever thank you? Your dress makes me feel almost worthy of my brave husband.'

Hélène explained Josh's situation to her grandmother and Mireille replied earnestly. 'She says in that case she is even more pleased that you should wear her dress for your wedding,' translated Hélène. 'You will both have married men who were courageous enough to fight for their countries.'

'You've all been so wonderful! I wish my mum could have been here to see this. She died when I was six, and on a day like tomorrow I know I'm going to miss her with all my heart. Dad will be walking me up the aisle, but I wonder if I could ask you another favour. Would you all come to my wedding and be my family? You and Thomas too, Sara?'

'Oh, Pippa.' Sara hugged her gently, being careful not to crumple the delicate silk. 'It would be an honour.'

Back at the château, they smuggled the dress into the cottage. 'Let's keep it a complete secret until the moment you walk into the chapel and knock them all for six!' suggested Sara. 'That way, even the groom won't see the dress before your big day, as is the tradition. And speaking of traditions, let's see: you've got the something old now – I think a vintage Dior dress fits the bill perfectly on that front; and your wedding shoes are the something new.'

'And I've got some pale blue underwear that I was going to wear for my something blue. That was in the bag with the shoes as well.'

'Well, in that case, can I lend you this? I think it might go really well with the dress.' Sara opened her jewellery box and fished out a velvet bag.

With big eyes, Pippa carefully drew out the pearls that it contained, a triple-stranded necklace with a diamond clasp. Sara fastened it around her slender neck and turned her round to look at herself in the mirror. 'It belonged to my grandmother. So there you go – something borrowed. Now you're all set.' Pippa's eyes sparkled even more brightly than the brilliant-cut diamonds in the clasp's setting. 'Now, don't you go crying again,' admonished Sara, taking out a tissue and blotting her own eyes. 'We're both going to have red blotches otherwise, and that's the last thing a bride wants for her big day. Go and tell Josh that everything's sorted, but don't give anything away. You're going to knock the socks off the lot of them – your mother-in-law included – when you make your entrance!'

'Oh, and just before you go, there's one more thing I wanted to ask you,' Sara continued. 'How would you feel about having a little extra media coverage of your wedding?' She fished her mobile phone out of her handbag and scrolled through the contacts list. 'Here we are. Nicola Carter . . . Let's see if she's as good as her word.'

◆ ◆ ◆

It was one of those sublime September afternoons, the softening summer light straight out of a painting by Monet or Cézanne. The wedding guests staying at hotels and bed and breakfasts in the surrounding area arrived first, making their way along the pathways lined with lavender and floating gaura flowers like clouds of white butterflies, before filing into the cool hush of the chapel. Each group paused between the tall cypress trees that flanked the chapel's portico to pose for photographs. Henri Dupont snapped away, entirely focused on the job in hand for once, as the editor herself from *Social Style* magazine stood at his elbow, directing the shots and making notes of names and designer outfits.

Then the members of the Cavendish family who had been staying in the château processed in and took their places in the front pews, which had 'reserved' signs taped to them. An usher came and whispered tactfully in the ear of cousin Ed and his rather horsey girlfriend, Camilla, when they seated themselves on the 'bride's side' at the front. 'But I thought Aunt Delia said she doesn't have any family,' Ed protested, a little too loudly. The usher whispered again and so the pair moved across, somewhat reluctantly, to a pew further back.

Delia and Henry processed in, the mother of the groom a vision in cerise with a matching hat, roughly the size and shape of the Starship *Enterprise*, pinned at a rakish angle to one side of her head. Mrs Cavendish gave a distinctly regal wave as she came up the aisle on her husband's arm, nodding graciously, if a little gingerly to ensure that her headgear stayed put. Sara had overheard her earlier telling one of the guests that it really was *most* gratifying that *Social Style* had heard about the wedding and sent Nicola Carter herself over specially to cover it for a feature they were doing on 'Weddings of The Season'. She was almost bursting out of her shot-silk jacket with pride and excitement.

There was a sudden burst of cheers from the ushers outside, debonair in their morning suits, and the assembled company craned their necks to see Josh and his best man, Will, being welcomed at the chapel door. They both looked splendid in their scarlet uniforms, Josh's enhanced even further by a row of medals. Will pushed the wheelchair slowly up the aisle, the groom's progress impeded by the handshakes and hugs and claps on the back that the guests bestowed on him as he passed.

And then, quietly and with dignity, a small group entered the chapel and an usher led them to the remaining reserved seats at the front. The bride's surrogate family – comprising the ancient Mireille Thibault, wearing an elegantly tailored suit, as well as the Héls Belles and their parents, and Karen and Antoine, all dressed in their Sunday best – filled the front pew across from the Cavendishes. Delia Cavendish looked surprised and sniffed disapprovingly, but managed a chilly nod of the flying-saucer hat as Mireille smiled serenely at her from across the aisle.

The chapel fell quiet, with a hush of expectation. The sound of light footsteps and soft voices, and a flurry of shutter snaps from a camera, could be heard just beyond the doorway in the golden sunlight as the bridal party arrived.

Outside the chapel, Sara gently pulled a fold of the skirt into place. She held Pippa at arm's length. 'You look just perfect,' she whispered. And then with a shake of Mr Hall's hand and a warm hug for his lovely daughter, Sara and Thomas wished them good luck and, hand in hand, slipped into the chapel and up the aisle to take their places next to the Thibaults.

As the music started and the bride entered, there was a series of gasps.

Firstly, the assembled company drew breath collectively at the sight of the beautiful girl – a vision of elegance and radiance in a vintage Dior wedding dress – as she walked up the aisle on her father's arm. Mrs Cavendish's jaw dropped visibly as Pippa drew level with the front pews.

And then the congregation gasped again, accompanied by a flurry of handkerchiefs and tissues being pulled from sleeves, pockets and handbags, at the sight of the groom, who, with a helping hand from his best man, rose to his feet and held out his arms to greet his lovely bride as she reached his side.

Chapter 12

THE BEGINNING

The phone echoed shrilly through the château and Sara hurried to the kitchen to answer it. 'Yes . . . yes, of course. I'll be pleased to send you the details. Could you spell that for me, please? Next Easter? I'll take a look in the diary and email you the dates we have free. Of course . . . that will be fine. I've made a note. Yes . . . Thank you so much for calling.'

'Another one?' Karen grinned, shaking out the duvet whose cover she'd just removed.

'Yup. At this rate, next season's going to end up being several weeks longer. I hope you weren't planning on taking any holidays next year! Coffee time?'

Back in the kitchen, Karen picked up the latest issue of *Social Style* magazine again, poring over the glossy pages. 'It's a great photo of you all. And look, Henri Dupont even gets a credit – he'll be dining out on that one for the rest of the year!'

> Pictured is *Social Style* magazine's Bride of the Year, Pippa Cavendish. The wedding took place at Château Bellevue de Coulliac in south-west

France on the 8th of September. The Groom was Captain Joshua Cavendish of the First Battalion of the Queen's Infantry. The Bride wore a vintage Christian Dior wedding gown and was given away by her father, Mr David Hall. Front row l-r: Miss Hélène Thibault, Miss Sara Cox, Mr Thomas Cortini, Mrs Mireille Thibault, Mr David Hall, Captain and Mrs Joshua Cavendish, Mr and Mrs Henry Cavendish, Miss Héloise Thibault, Mr Antoine Forestier. See page 142 for further coverage, in our feature on the Weddings of The Season.

◆ ◆ ◆

Sara came out of the cottage carrying a box of leftover cartons of cereal and pots of jam. She paused in the peace of the late September morning to take a deep breath of the early autumn air. It had a hint of ripeness to it, a faint truffle scent of falling leaves and damp earth, mingling with the perfume of the sun-warmed grapes on the vines, almost ready for the harvest. From the woodland in the valley below the château, a green woodpecker's manic cackle echoed between the trees.

As she made her way across to the kitchen, Thomas stuck his head round the doorway of the barn. 'Ah, Sara, there you are! Could you come in here for a second?' She put the box down on the path and stepped into the cool twilight of the high-beamed room, which had resounded with the sound of disco beats on all those summer Saturday nights, but was now silent.

Thomas was at the decks. 'I've been saving the last dance for you. Wait there a moment! Don't move . . .'

He flicked a switch on the wall and the glitter ball began to revolve, casting shooting stars on to the walls and floor. He pushed a button on the sound system and then walked across to where Sara stood in the starlight, a scattering of confetti at her feet. 'Mam'selle Sara, I do believe they're playing our song. May I have the pleasure?' asked Thomas, and she stepped into his arms.

As Elvis began to sing, Thomas held her close and they started to dance.

And as they swayed together, it seemed to Sara that in that moment they stood still, at the perfect centre of the universe, the sun, moon and stars orbiting about them. She heard Eliane's voice: 'Your château is built on love, Sara. Love and happiness. No matter what sadness has happened here too. Always remember that.'

And she thought of each of the couples who had danced here before them, wondering whether they had felt the same way. She thought of Niamh, her black eye not mattering one jot when she knew she was so well loved by Keiran and by her family; she remembered Matthew and Hamish, safe in the knowledge that, together, they could be their own true selves and be loved all the more for it; she smiled as she thought of Patti and Thorne, so sure of what really mattered beneath the glitz and the glamour; and she heard Bill, saying 'love is the most important thing there is, at any age'. And finally she saw Pippa and Josh standing together in the chapel, if only for a moment, so determined and so strong in the knowledge that they could make it together, no matter what obstacles life threw their way.

Until then, she'd thought of each wedding as a fairy-tale ending, the happy-ever-after moment for each couple. But now she realised that the exact opposite was true. Each wedding was a fairy-tale beginning – a moment of celebration, carefully choreographed by the supporting cast of her and her team, by the wedding planners, the family members and the good friends, before the ups and downs of real life began again.

Thomas's lips brushed her hair as he kissed her softly. And in that moment, it was as if the thicket of thorns that had grown around her heart to protect it died back, melting away and leaving only a sense of peace and clarity in its place: a feeling she hadn't had since she was a child.

Another memory came into her head, of a little girl with dark, glossy hair, walking safely between her parents, kicking up the leaves from the floor of a beech wood in the autumn; the child was wearing a red woollen duffel coat – she remembered how proud she'd been of being able to fasten the wooden toggles by herself – and walked in a pool of golden light, oblivious to the darkness, the evil spells and the big, bad wolves that lurked behind the trees on the path ahead, safe in the knowledge that she, too, was loved.

The music came to an end, but Thomas stood there a little longer, holding her. 'And I can't help falling in love with you,' he whispered into her ear, echoing the words of the song. 'In fact, I was wondering . . . Being business partners is all very well, but it really doesn't take into account the fact that I love you, body and soul, with all my heart. So, Sara, my beautiful Boss, would you make me the happiest man alive by agreeing to be my wife as well?'

She smiled up at him and then stood on tiptoe to kiss him, resting her cheek against his shoulder for a moment. 'For better, for worse?'

'With you, there is only better. No worse.'

'For richer, for poorer?'

'It's our love that makes us rich.'

'Until death do us part?'

'A love such as ours? We've already proved it would take more than death. I want to spend the rest of my life with you. I realised that as I lost consciousness: I was terrified, but then I looked into your eyes and I felt an amazing sense of peace, and I knew that if the last thing I saw of this Earth was your face, then I would die happy.'

She gazed deep into his eyes, reading the truth of the love that was written there. A love strong enough to bathe her in a pool of golden light and keep at bay whatever darkness lay beyond the trees. Eliane's voice came back to her once more. 'Remember, Sara, even in the darkest of times, love will light the way. Always.'

'Yes,' she said. 'Of course, yes.'

His slow smile spread across his face like the sunrise on a summer's day, and he kissed her. And then he stepped back and, with a sweep of his arm, said, 'Come on then, Boss. Time to go and reclaim the throne in your fairy-tale castle.'

And, taking her arm in his, he walked beside her, back towards the ancient château sitting on a hilltop among the vines, high above a golden river.

– The End –

ACKNOWLEDGEMENTS

This book is one of the trio in the *Escape to France* series. It was first published as *The French for Always*. But this edition, renamed *The Season of Dreams*, is published by the Lake Union team at Amazon Publishing and I am most grateful for their encouragement and input, as well as for the opportunity to revise some sections of the original manuscript and bring it up to date.

If you've enjoyed meeting Eliane and Mireille and would like to get to know them better, their lives during the war years are explored in *The Beekeeper's Promise* and *The Dressmaker's Gift*. And if you're intrigued to know the answer to the mystery of the initials carved on the cellar wall, you'll find it in *The Beekeeper's Promise*.

Some of the places mentioned here do exist and you'll find them on any good map; others, such as the village of Coulliac, are figments of my imagination. I was fortunate to once live in a part of the world where there are many beautiful châteaux, and some of them are the venues for weddings. Château Bellevue de Coulliac, however, is not based on any of them and is entirely fictitious; any resemblances to real people or places are purely coincidental. The underlying limestone, which is the bedrock of much of this part of France, is famous for its tunnels and caves; if you're intrigued and would like to visit some, then the underground church of Saint-Émilion and the caves around Les Eyzies (which include the world-famous prehistoric paintings of Lascaux) are magical and fascinating places.

Huge thanks to my agent, Madeleine Milburn, and to Liv Maidment and the rest of the team at the Madeleine Milburn Agency. And to the team at Amazon Publishing – Victoria Oundjian, Sammia Hamer, Mike Jones, Jenni Davis, Swati Gamble, Bekah Graham and Nicole Wagner.

I'm immensely grateful to Joan Harcourt for her long-distance support and encouragement early on in my writing career (and for Thomas's slow smile); thank you to my goddaughter, Nixy, and her mother, Pippa, for letting me borrow their names. Thanks and huge respect to James Valpy and Tracy Metz for the insights into life on tour and the technical details of sound and lighting. Thanks to Alastair Valpy for the insights into being a student bartender, and to Kay Eddy, who knows how much hard work is involved behind the scenes in organising dream weddings.

And finally, love and thanks to my family and friends, who always make me smile.

READ ON FOR AN EXTRACT
FROM FIONA VALPY'S
THE RECIPE FOR HOPE

We're sitting at Rose's kitchen table in the aftermath of the final book club meeting of the year, the last Friday in November. The others have all left, making their way home to their families, looking forward to their busy weekends. But I'm lingering in the bright warmth of Rose's kitchen, pretending to make myself useful collecting up glasses and plates, reluctant to go back and push open the door to my own darkened house, knowing that its emptiness will ring loud in my ears. Avoiding the sad silence of the rooms where my grief lives behind their shut doors, decomposing quietly until it loses enough of its radioactive power to be handled safely. How many half-lives will that be, I wonder?

Rose's husband, Max, pokes his head round the doorway. 'Is it safe to come out yet?' He'd been banished to his study for the evening, the book club being a girls-only affair, and now he's come to claim his reward from the dishes of leftovers that clutter the kitchen table. He gives me a hug. 'How's my favourite Yankee redhead? And is there any of your quiche left, Evie? Oh, good,' he sighs, picking up a slice and taking a bite. 'Delicious as ever.'

'I know,' Rose nods, breaking off the corner of the last slice left in the dish and savouring the rich mix of Comté cheese and smoked bacon. 'You've given me the recipe, but it never tastes as good when I make it. Must be your French-Irish-American *je ne sais quoi*.' She raises her glass with a flourish. '*Santé!* Or should that be *Sláinte?*'

She pours some more wine into my glass and then tips the dregs into her own, raising it to the light so that it gleams with a soft ruby glow. Her expression is thoughtful. 'When are you going to think about getting back in the saddle again, Evie? Your talent's going to waste, you know. There must be restaurants out there that would snap you up. Or maybe you could try your hand at writing a few articles for one of the cookery magazines?'

'Don't push her, Rose.' Max reaches over to pat my arm. 'All in good time, after the year she's had.'

I smile at him, thankful for his kindness. By now, most people have stopped being kind, or openly so at least. They've moved on with their own lives, leaving me stuck at the point where mine stopped. I feel like I'm watching them all disappearing over the horizon without a backward glance as I stand forlornly, mired here in the quicksand of my grief, weighted down by my anger.

Not waving, but drowning.

'I've promised myself I'll get back on to it in the New Year. There's no point now with December just round the corner. I'll get through Christmas and then see.' And, while I'm trying to keep my tone light and even, I confess I'm terrified at the prospect: I don't know yet whether I'm going to stay on in London or move back to Boston. Such big decisions require energy and I'm fresh out of that right now. I hope I sound more upbeat than I feel, but Rose fixes me with her gimlet gaze, the one she uses to such good effect, to see through the surface veneer of fake cheerfulness to the truth underneath.

'Ah, yes, and speaking of Christmas, what are your plans? Max and I would be delighted if you would come and spend the day with us. I promise not to make you cook a thing.'

Max looks a little crestfallen. 'Or, well, maybe just one of your pies if you felt like it?' he suggests. 'I've never really liked Christmas pudding and your blueberry one is my absolute favourite. Or what's that upside-down apple thing with the caramel?'

'*Tarte Tatin*?'

'That's the one. Delicious!'

'Back off, Max,' Rose warns, laughing, although I'm grateful she's protecting me as usual. 'She doesn't have to cook anything.'

I sigh, reluctant to think about Christmas at all. All those memories of last year, coming home from the hospital on Christmas Eve to a houseful of shattered dreams; Will unable to bring himself to look at the shadows of pain and grief etched on to my face as he set my overnight case down carefully on the bed, treading cautiously, as if we might both break into a thousand pieces at any sudden move. He'd closed the door softly behind him and left me to unpack. I was still sitting there, the case unopened beside me, when he came back to check on me an hour later.

I wasn't angry with him then, only stunned and shocked with grief.

The anger came later.

'That's really kind. I just don't know . . . I'm still wondering whether I shouldn't go back to the States. Though it feels kind of cowardly to run away.'

In fact, the real reason I'm even thinking twice about it is because I can't face my mother's determined cheerfulness, her efforts to involve me in the childbirth charity she's now fundraising for, which is typical of her way of coping; she's always been a doer, strong enough to face anything head-on and find a way to move forward. She won't be able to understand why I can't do the same.

That, and the fact that my sister, Tess, is seven months pregnant: the exact same stage I was when it happened, at Christmas last year. None of us is saying it, but I know they're holding their breath, praying that her baby will make it through, even though there's no earthly reason why it shouldn't.

But then there was no earthly reason why my baby's heart stopped beating. Just one of those things, they said . . .

I try to summon a smile for Rose and Max and their invitation. 'I don't know – it's just that Will's face is going to be everywhere here with this new TV series. Last week I had to do a body swerve in the supermarket when I came face to face with a copy of the *Radio Times*.'

The magazine trumpeted 'Will Brooke's Delicious December Dining', his face beaming out at me from the front cover. Flustered by a surge of conflicting emotions, I'd steered my trolley into a festive stack (already!) of tins of Danish butter cookies, sending them clattering across the floor. I still feel guilty about leaving them there. I'd stumbled out of the shop and sat shaking in my car, my hands fumbling as I tried to fit the key into the ignition.

Rose takes my hand, her expression one of tender concern. Uh-oh, something's up: she's not usually the sentimental type. I brace myself.

'Evie, I don't know if you've seen this?' She pulls a gossip magazine out from under a pile of glossier ones. I shake my head. 'I thought not. Well, I think you do need to see it before anyone else mentions it.' She turns to a two-page spread, where Will's face beams out at me again. 'Will Power!' shouts the headline. 'Celebrity chef Will Brooke talks about his tragic loss and new beginnings as he launches his series of festive cookery programmes.' Rose sits back, allowing me time to scan the article and take it all in. It's mostly pictures of him in his apron, wielding a kitchen knife and presenting a steaming pot pie – my grandmother's recipe, I note, with my cranberry glaze, which, though I do say so myself, looks very attractive. But the final picture is a less posed one, a fuzzy shot of him snapped in the street with his arm around the shoulder of a pretty blonde. 'Something's cooking: we can reveal Will's mystery girl is Stephanie Wallis, an assistant on the new show.'

My stomach knots as I take in the photo and the chatty text beneath it. And then I read, 'Brave Will is trying to put the tragedy of losing the baby behind him and focus on his future. As he so rightly says, the show must go on!'

I fold the magazine shut, feeling nauseous, and place it very carefully on the table in front of me. Rose and Max are sitting on either side, watching me intently, and Rose puts a hand on my arm again. Her touch brings me to. I turn to look at her, trying to summon a scornful smile at this ridiculous article in this trashy magazine. But my face won't behave the way I want it to. Of its own accord, it crumples and collapses. And Rose pulls me to her as I begin to sob uncontrollably. 'At last,' she says, matter-of-factly. 'I was wondering if you were *ever* going to cry.'

It's true, it's the first time I've cried in a long, long while; I thought I'd gotten pretty good at covering my true feelings, but this has caught me unawares. So it takes me a bit of time to regain control and be able to take the Kleenex Max is offering me and blow my nose. I look at Rose's face and see that she, too, has tears in her eyes.

She knows how I feel because she was there, through the whole terrible ordeal. This must be conjuring up painful memories for her as well. She was the one who came to the hospital when I called her because Will was up in Manchester and too busy with the filming of *On Your Marks, Get Set, Cook!*, which he was hoping would lead to bigger and better things. Admittedly, it was my own fault too. I told him not to rush back. After all, by then there was nothing he could do; there was no heartbeat, the baby was gone. And the hospital said they'd leave it for a day or two before they induced my labour. I should just go home and let it sink in; there was no rush. So, when I told him this, Will said, 'Okay, if you're absolutely sure, Evie. I'll be home tomorrow night anyway. And if you've got Rose there with you for the time being . . .' How was either of us to know the contractions would start spontaneously that night, too late for him to get a train or hire a car? So that, by the time he arrived at the hospital, all that was left for him to do was to hold our child, just that once, and then bring me home. Back to a house that felt as empty and sad as I did myself.

'Sorry, Evie,' Rose says.

'That's okay. Thank you for showing me. Better that I know what's out there. But, you know, I'm just not sure I can do it.' I start to cry again, blotting my eyes with the soggy tissue. 'I have to get away. I can't stay here with all this' – I wave a hand at the magazine – 'but I can't go home to America either. I want to cancel Christmas and crawl away into a cave somewhere where I can be on my own. I just can't face the fun and the glitz and all the features about Delicious Dining and Festive Feasts. You're so kind to invite me to join you, but it'd ruin it for all of you, tiptoeing around me in case something sets me off again. I have to get away. But there's nowhere for me to go.' My voice shakes with fear and wretchedness, and fury at Will and his mystery girl, and – okay, okay, I admit it – self-pity.

Rose and Max exchange a glance and he nods. 'We thought that might be the case.' Rose pats my hand again. 'So we've come up with a Plan B. Why don't you go and spend Christmas in the house in France? You can take yourself off there for some peace and some space and have a complete break. It's not so far to go that you'll be stuck if you change your mind and you want to come back to London and spend Christmas with us after all, but you'll be able to escape the media circus there. And you know how you love French cuisine. Who knows, it might do you good to get back to your roots. Maybe you could even start researching an article or two.'

I shake my head. I've definitely lost my cooking mojo and, right now, the last thing I want to think about is facing up to the collapse of my career, let alone the rest of my life.

Max pats my other hand. 'You don't have to force yourself to do anything, Evie. Just take some time out. Plonk yourself down there with a few bottles of the local wine and perhaps an occasional quiche.' Max reaches out his hand for the remainder of the last slice and raises it in a jaunty salute. 'Use it as a time to recharge your batteries. Things might look clearer from a distance. And at the very least you'll be spared the shopping frenzy and the continuous tacky Christmas music, and the conspicuous consumption and the completely crap weather that we'll be bombarded with here. In fact, come to think of it, it sounds quite tempting. Perhaps I'll come and join you.' The pastry crust crumbles as he sinks his teeth into it, scattering golden crumbs down his shirt front.

'In your dreams, Max Morgan!' retorts Rose. 'I know you'd far rather be in France with your favourite American than back here in grey London with your stressed-out harridan of a wife and your children arguing with you about which film to watch on the telly, but you're staying here.'

'Ah, well, since you put it like that . . . And a very merry Christmas to you too, my darling!' Max kisses her fondly on the top of her head as he carries the now empty quiche dish over to the sink.

I sit and think, Rose's offer sinking in slowly. It does sound tempting. And escaping would be a neat solution to my woes. I glance at the gossip magazine again. In fact . . . 'How soon could I go?'

Rose follows my gaze and then beams at me. 'Why, as soon as you like! The house is sitting empty. It's yours for as long as you want it.'

I wipe the mascara from under my eyes and blow my nose again. 'Could I maybe go next week? Plan on spending the whole of December there?'

'Of course you can, my darling . . . and with not a Festive Feast in sight!'

I manage to summon a watery grin and pick up the magazine again. 'Oh, well, at least he gives me a mention.' I read aloud: '"Will and his ex-wife opened the highly successful Brooke's Bistro five years ago but sold the business last year as Will's career took off. 'My wife, Evie, was the wind beneath my wings,' explains Will, 'but sadly we've grown apart.'" I suppose it's better than nothing,' I sigh, hoping for sympathy. I should have known better.

Rose guffaws. 'And just when did the wind beneath his wings turn into the doormat beneath his feet, might I ask? Honestly, Evie, you were always the true talent in the partnership and Will knows that. I give him a year. He'll soon realise how much he needs you and your recipes once the honeymoon period wears off. And by that time I hope you'll have realised it yourself and be back in the kitchen, getting the recognition you deserve in your own right. And then he'll be sorry.' Her expression softens as I wipe another tear away. 'Come on, love, you just need a bit more time, that's all. Life happens, you know? Of course you're battered and bruised right now, who wouldn't be? But I promise you, you will come out the other side of this and be stronger than before. I'm so glad you're going to France. It'll be the perfect break, a chance to get some perspective on what you want to do next.'

I nod. 'You're right. And you know what? Life sure as hell happens, but at least this year I can make sure Christmas won't. Not for me, at least. And for that I am truly grateful to you both.'

'You sure you'll be okay?' Rose asks as she stands in the doorway to see me out. She hugs me. 'Come straight back if you don't want to be in the house alone.'

'I'm fine. Got a busy weekend ahead of me. I'm off to France, dontcha know, and I've got some serious packing to do. Anyway, don't worry – if I find myself at loose ends, there's always the Playbook!'

Rose and I are agreed that *Silver Linings Playbook* is our very favourite movie of all time. Currently, at least: we reserve the right to replace it at some future point, just as it replaced *Dirty Dancing* (Rose's long-standing choice) and *It's Complicated* (mine, because of the scene with the *croque monsieurs* as well as the one with Alec Baldwin and the webcam). But, for the time being, the Playbook, as we like to refer to it, is our favourite for the following three reasons:

Bradley Cooper is gorgeous.

The two main characters have both been made crazy by grief and anger and, for them as for me, this craziness feels more normal and more rational than the so-called sanity of everyone else in the world.

Bradley Cooper is gorgeous.

I suspect in Rose's case only reasons (1) and (3) apply.

A late-fall fog hangs in the air as I walk back through the lamplit streets, my heels tapping on the London sidewalk with new purpose. Now, instead of dreading the blankness of the weekend that stretches before me, I'm looking forward to it. I have work to do: I need to book my crossing, do my packing, tidy the house. Plan my escape back to my beloved France. My heart lifts as I realise I can even swing by Paris on the way down. Am I ready for that walk down memory lane? I ask myself. And, to my surprise, I think maybe I am. I can't wait to step back to a time before sadness and fear, when life was there for the taking.

It was thanks to my darling grandmother, Mamie Lucie, and her bequest to me of the notebook full of recipes and enough money for a ticket across the Atlantic, that the world suddenly opened up before me and became, as the saying goes, my *huître*. Memories flood back to me as I walk home through the damp streets: my first day at the cookery school, with its bright, spotlessly clean counters and sets of gleaming utensils at each station, the air smelling faintly – like the best restaurants do – of butter and the subtle undertones of dill and white wine from the fish dish that the students had been cooking that morning; an evening in a bar with my fellow students from the four corners of the world, an exciting mix of cultures, complexions, accents, all of us laughing as English Will did his impersonation of the chef, Monsieur Charles, tasting the bouillon and declaring it an 'abomination'. We nicknamed him 'Prince William' because he did bear a passing resemblance to the second in line to the British throne with his good looks and pol-ished manners. He had charisma, even then, and was always the star of the show.

And then there are those other, more private memories: Will's eyes meeting mine above the rim of my wine glass, something click-ing into place, a connection, a certainty; lying together, tangled in the sheets, in my tiny one-room apartment high up among the Parisian rooftops; Will standing on the bed to push open the roof light, craning his head and saying, 'Hey! You can even see the Eiffel Tower from here!' then holding me steady as I joined him on tip-toes on the shifting, lumpy mattress and we gazed out across a pet-rified forest of redundant chimney pots and TV antennas to where the lights of Paris's most iconic landmark twinkled and winked at us. As if it was sharing in our joy and our exhilaration at having found each other in the city of love.

I reach the high street, my stream of thoughts interrupted by the necessity of crossing the busy stream of London traffic. On the other side I hesitate, choosing which route to take back to the house. Recently, I've been taking the longer way round, sticking to the main streets and avoiding the cut-through where the bistro used to be. But tonight, in my newfound glow of positivity, I decide to be brave and so I turn the toes of my boots in the direction of the antique shops and quirkier boutiques.

'*Fabio's Ristorante Italiano*' the new sign reads, its red neon infusing the November fog with a garish chemical glow. 'Book your Christmas lunch now!' is scrawled on a chalkboard outside. 'Special menu!' I walk on, picking up the pace as I try not to remember how it used to be when the sign read 'Brooke's Bistro' in old-gold lettering. I would set each table with soft linens and a little vase of fresh flowers, and write the daily menu of dishes made from whatever produce was fresh and in season on that same chalkboard.

I make it past, my heart rate quickening a bit, I note, but nothing too much more overwhelming than that. Progress. A small triumph.

But my sense of achievement falters and then sputters out like a candle drowning in its own wax as I reach my front door and grope in the bottom of my purse for the keys.

'*France!*' I whisper to myself. '*Focus on that. Nothing else.*'

I push the door open, stepping into the hushed warmth of the hallway and the silent sadness of this space that should have been filled with my husband's welcoming arms and the gurgling smiles of our baby daughter.

Should-a, would-a, could-a. All those might-have-beens. Some of the emptiest words there are.

I wipe my feet on the mat before easing off my boots, and as I do, Rose's comment comes back to me. *And just when did the wind beneath his wings become the doormat beneath his feet?* A throwaway remark, but one that stings a little, I have to admit. The truth hurts, as they say.

I set my boots neatly side by side beneath the coat hooks. As I straighten up, I can't help brushing my fingers over the faded fabric of an old jacket of Will's that he's left behind, the elbows rubbed shiny with wear, un-needed in his newer, more glamorous life. Was it my fault he left? Was it my anger that drove him away? Or was it his own guilt?

The bistro had been a true partnership, each of us bringing our own particular skills to the business. I supplied the ideas for menus and he had the strength and the unflagging energy that the gruelling daily routine in the kitchen demanded. At first we worked side by side, Will as head chef while I did the baking, preparing our trademark home-made breads and pastries, and ran the front of house. The most popular dish on the lunch menu was always my wheaten soda bread (in homage to my Irish roots), spread thick with unsalted French butter and served with the soup of the day: true comfort food and the best and simplest kind of fusion cuisine.

Then, when I discovered I was pregnant – a miracle, so soon after we decided to start trying, because the business was on solid foundations, its popularity starting to soar – I began to struggle to keep up with the schedule. I was exhausted, battling with the nausea as the morning sickness hit me hard. 'Never mind,' Will had reassured me. 'You rest. We can afford the extra staff to cover your areas. Just do the lunchtime shifts, if you're up to it.'

I thought I'd get my energy back after the first trimester. After all, that's how it's supposed to be, isn't it? Women glowing with pregnancy, radiating an abundance of serene energy as they morph into motherhood? Only not in my case. The nausea never really abated, which meant that being around food became a torture instead of the joy it used to be. First I went off coffee – even the smell of it made my stomach heave; the thought of a glass of wine brought acid surging into my throat; the sight of Will filleting mackerel made me gag; and the mere idea of whipping a bowl of cream had my insides lurching like a butter churn. All of which is a bit of a handicap when you work in a restaurant.

I couldn't bow out completely though. I cared too passionately about the bistro (my other baby!) so I'd drag myself in to help set up for lunch and dinner and chalk the *plat du jour* on the board, swallowing hard. Some days, when I felt a little stronger, I'd get back into the kitchen, adding my trademark touches to certain dishes, suggesting recipes to Will depending on what fresh produce we had that day. And back home I'd experiment with new recipes, digging into Mamie Lucie's tattered notebook and deciphering her spidery handwriting, with frequent consultations of my French dictionary whenever I came across an ingredient or an instruction that I wasn't sure of. Trying to contribute to the bistro's menu as best I could.

And then came the day when, as I was arranging the vase of flowers for the front desk (one of the few chores that I still positively enjoyed), I felt that first tiny movement inside of me. Not the churning of my gut, but something else, deep inside my belly. A flutter, as delicate and persistent as the wings of a butterfly against a windowpane: my baby moving, kicking her tiny heels against the walls that confined her. I froze. Then placed my hand over the spot, willing her to do it again. And she did. As if she heard me ask the question, and she kicked back in reply.

And in that moment my heart was locked to hers with a strength so fierce that it took my breath away.

I spoke to her constantly from then on. I'd tell her about the day's menu as I wrote it out and she'd drum her heels approvingly; I'd breathe deep the scent of the white trumpet-like lilies on the front desk as I passed, hoping their perfume would infuse my bloodstream so that she would be surrounded by it too; and I'd gently caress my ballooning belly, calling to Will to come and feel the butterfly movements as our daughter stretched and flexed and reached out to us from the dark warmth of her cocoon.

For me, though, the radiant stage never materialised. My back ached, and I grew even more exhausted as the months rolled slowly by. I longed for the day when our baby would be born, finally separate from me so that I could try to regain some kind of balance in my life, freed at last from the dense fog of sick exhaustion that smothered me throughout my pregnancy. And I'll admit, I feel overwhelmed with guilt now, remembering this. I'd give anything to have her still moving in my belly. Unconsciously, I put a hand on the flat front of my jeans, my stomach concave between the sharply jutting hipbones. Empty. Realising, I jerk my hand away, as though from the scalding rim of a hot pan.

The silence in the house closes in around me like a soft blanket.

I prefer being alone these days. Because, strictly between you and me, ever since last Christmas Eve I've been living two lives. One involves silence and distance and pain and loss. It's a lonely life, where my husband has left me, unable to bear the weight of my grief on top of his own; unable to soothe my anger and his guilt; unable to accept that I can't move on when he can.

It's reality.

My second life, which runs on a parallel track, is an imaginary one, and I escape into it whenever I can. Because it's filled with light and noise and love. In it, Will is still here and our beautiful baby daughter is now nearly a year old; it's a world where I am sleep-deprived (instead of in the constant state of medicinally induced hibernation that I sink into in my real life, popping a pill and retreating into blessed oblivion whenever I can); I walk up and down in the nursery when the rest of the world is asleep, holding her against my heart, stroking her back, soothing her and singing her lullabies, not minding that she won't go back to sleep, because her every breath, her every cry, is proof she's alive. In this other life, I deal cheerfully with dirty nappies, teething and tantrums, late night feeds and early morning wake-up calls; I plan her first Christmas – our first Christmas as a family – and her first birthday party; I chat to my sister, Tess, every day just like we used to do, offering her my sympathy and advice as her own pregnancy progresses, looking forward to the day when our children will be favourite cousins and spend magical summer holidays together at the lake house in New Hampshire.

You have to admit, it's a much nicer life than the real one.

So, when I'm alone, I allow myself to go there sometimes, luxuriating in the fantasy. Because, don't worry, I *do* know it's a fantasy. I've not yet taken to playing with dolls and pushing an empty stroller through the streets, cooing to my imaginary baby. It's my secret craziness, my own *Silver Linings Playbook*, where everything has turned out just fine in the end and Will and I are busy living in our own happy-ever-after.

Sad, isn't it, my private parallel universe? A refuge for my broken heart; a refuge from my grief.

The hall clock chimes. Shocked out of my reverie, I look at my boots sitting there side by side and then catch a glimpse of my face in the hallway mirror. My skin is too pale and the dark half-moon shadows beneath my eyes stand out stark against it. I run a hand through my hair, trying to smooth the copper curls, which have gone a little frizzy, as usual, in the damp London air.

I go upstairs to the bathroom, the two his-and-hers sinks mocking me as I rummage in the cabinet for the foil pack of pills. The doctor prescribed these antidepressants when I got to the stage of being unable to haul my sorry carcass out of bed for several days at a stretch. They make me feel a little foggy, removed from reality, but then isn't that the point? Under the unforgiving glare of the bathroom lights, my reflection seems too far away, as though it, too, has disconnected itself from me and my grief.

I guess you know you are really and truly alone when even your own reflection deserts you.

I sway a little, gripping the side of the sink to try to steady the faint giddiness as the pills kick in.

'*France*,' I whisper to myself again. A faint glimmer of light at the end of a very long, very dark, very lonely tunnel.

ABOUT THE AUTHOR

Photo credit: Willow Findlay

Fiona is an acclaimed number one bestselling author whose books have sold over a million copies and been translated into more than twenty languages worldwide. She draws inspiration from the stories of strong women, especially during the years of World War Two, and her meticulous historical research enriches her writing with an evocative sense of time and place.

For more information, to sign up for updates or to get in touch, please visit www.fionavalpy.com.